CROOKED HOUSE

AGATHA CHRISTIE is known throughout the world as the Queen of Crime. Her seventy-seven detective novels and books of stories have been translated into every major language, and her sales are calculated in tens of millions.

She began writing at the end of the First World War, when she created Hercule Poirot, the little Belgian detective with the egg-shaped head and the passion for order – the most popular sleuth in fiction since Sherlock Holmes. Poirot, fluffy Miss Marple and her other detectives have appeared in the films, radio programmes and stage plays based on her books.

Agatha Christie also wrote six romantic novels under the pseudonym Mary Westmacott, several plays and a book of poems; as well, she assisted her archaeologist husband Sir Max Mallowan on many expeditions to the Near East.

Postern of Fate was the last book she wrote before her death in 1976, but since its publication William Collins has also published two books Agatha Christie wrote in the 1940s: *Curtain: Poirot's Last Case* in 1975 and *Sleeping Murder*, the last Miss Marple book in 1976.

Agatha Christie's *Autobiography* appeared in 1977.

AGATHA CHRISTIE

Crooked House

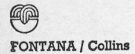

FONTANA / Collins

First published in 1949 by William Collins Sons & Co. Ltd
First issued in Fontana Books 1959
Twentieth Impression April 1980

© Agatha Christie Mallowan, 1948, 1949

Made and printed in Great Britain by
William Collins Sons & Co Ltd Glasgow

AUTHOR'S FOREWORD

This book is one of my own special favourites. I saved
it up for years, thinking about it, working it out,
saying to myself: 'One day, when I've plenty of time,
and want to really enjoy myself—I'll begin it!' I
should say that of one's output, five books are work
to one that is real pleasure. *Crooked House* was pure
pleasure. I often wonder whether people who read a
book can know if it has been hard work or a pleasure
to write? Again and again someone says to me: '*How
you must have enjoyed writing so and so!*' This
about a book that obstinately refused to come out
the way you wished, whose characters are sticky,
the plot needlessly involved, and the dialogue stilted
—or so you think yourself. But perhaps the author
isn't the best judge of his or her own work. However,
practically everybody has liked *Crooked House*, so I
am justified in my own belief that it is one of my best.

I don't know what put the Leonides family into my
head—they just came. Then, like Topsy 'they growed'.

I feel that I myself was only their scribe.

AGATHA CHRISTIE

I FIRST came to know Sophia Leonides in Egypt towards the end of the war. She held a fairly high administrative post in one of the Foreign Office departments out there. I knew her first in an official capacity, and I soon appreciated the efficiency that had brought her to the position she held, in spite of her youth (she was at that time just twenty-two).

Besides being extremely easy to look at, she had a clear mind and a dry sense of humour that I found very delightful. We became friends. She was a person whom it was extraordinarily easy to talk to and we enjoyed our dinners and occasional dances very much.

All this I knew; it was not until I was ordered East at the close of the European war that I knew something else—that I loved Sophia and that I wanted to marry her.

We were dining at Shepheard's when I made this discovery. It did not come to me with any shock of surprise, but more as the recognition of a fact with which I had been long familiar. I looked at her with new eyes—but I saw what I had already known for a long time. I liked everything I saw. The dark crisp hair that sprang up proudly from her forehead, the vivid blue eyes, the small square fighting chin, and the straight nose. I liked the well-cut light-grey tailor-made, and the crisp white shirt. She looked refreshingly English and that appealed to me strongly after three years without seeing my native land. Nobody, I thought, could be more English —and even as I was thinking exactly that, I suddenly wondered if, in fact, she was, or indeed could be, as English as she looked. Does the real thing ever have the perfection of a stage performance?

I realised that much and freely as we had talked together, discussing ideas, our likes and dislikes, the future, our immediate friends and acquaintances—Sophia had never mentioned her home or her family. She knew all about me (she was, as I have indicated, a good listener) but about her I knew nothing. She had, I supposed, the usual background, but she had never talked about it. And until this moment I had never realised the fact.

Sophia asked me what I was thinking about.

I replied truthfully: "You."

"I see," she said. And she sounded as though she did see.

"We may not meet again for a couple of years," I said. "I don't know when I shall get back to England. But as soon as I do get back, the first thing I shall do will be to come and see you and ask you to marry me."

She took it without batting an eyelash. She sat there, smoking, not looking at me.

For a moment or two I was nervous that she might not understand.

"Listen," I said. "The one thing I'm determined *not* to do, is to ask you to marry me now. That wouldn't work out anyway. First you might turn me down, and then I'd go off miserable and probably tie up with some ghastly woman just to restore my vanity. And if you didn't turn me down what could we do about it? Get married and part at once? Get engaged and settle down to a long waiting period? I couldn't stand your doing that. You might meet someone else and feel bound to be 'loyal' to me. We've been living in a queer hectic get-on-with-it-quickly atmosphere. Marriages and love affairs making and breaking all round us. I'd like to feel you'd gone home, free and independent, to look round you and size up the new post-war world and decide what you want out of it. What is between you and me, Sophia, has got to be *permanent*. I've no use for any other kind of marriage."

"No more have I," said Sophia.

"On the other hand," I said, "I think I'm entitled to let you know how I—well—how I feel."

"But without undue lyrical expression?" murmured Sophia.

"Darling—don't you understand? I've tried *not* to say I love you——"

She stopped me.

"I do understand, Charles. And I like your funny way of doing things. And you may come and see me when you come back—if you still want to——"

It was my turn to interrupt.

"There's no doubt about that."

"There's always a doubt about everything, Charles. There may always be some incalculable factor that upsets the apple-cart. For one thing, you don't know much about me, do you?"

"I don't even know where you live in England."

"I live at Swinly Dean."

I nodded at the mention of the well-known outer suburb of London which boasts three excellent golf courses for the city financier.

She added softly in a musing voice: "*In a little crooked house* . . ."

I must have looked slightly startled, for she seemed amused, and explained by elaborating the quotation. "'*And they all lived together in a little crooked house.*' That's us. Not really such a little house either. But definitely crooked—running to gables and half-timbering!"

"Are you one of a large family? Brothers and sisters?"

"One brother, one sister, a mother, a father, an uncle, an aunt by marriage, a grandfather, a great-aunt, and a step-grandmother."

"Good gracious!" I exclaimed, slightly overwhelmed.

She laughed.

"Of course we don't normally all live together. The war and blitzes have brought that about—but I don't know"—she frowned reflectively—"perhaps spiritually the family has always lived together—under my grandfather's eye and protection. He's rather a Person. my grandfather. He's over eighty, about four-foot ten, and everybody else looks rather dim beside him."

"He sounds interesting," I said.

"He is interesting He's a Greek from Smyrna. Aristide Leonides." She added. with a twinkle. "He's extremely rich."

"Will anybody be rich after this is over?"

"My grandfather will," said Sophia with assurance. "No soak-the-rich tactics would have any effect on him. He'd just soak the soakers.

"I wonder." she added, "if you'll like him?"

"Do you?" I asked.

"Better than anyone in the world," said Sophia.

II

It was over two years before I returned to England. They were not easy years. I wrote to Sophia and heard from her fairly frequently. Her letters, like mine, were not love letters. They were letters written to each other by close friends—they dealt with ideas and thoughts and with comments on the daily trend of life. Yet I know that as far as I was concerned, and I believed as far as Sophia was concerned too, our feelings for each other grew and strengthened.

I returned to England on a soft grey day in September. The leaves on the trees were golden in the evening light. There were playful gusts of wind. From the airfield I sent a telegram to Sophia.

"Just arrived back. Will you dine this evening Mario's nine o'clock Charles."

A couple of hours later I was sitting reading *The Times*; and scanning the Births, Marriages, and Deaths column my eye was caught by the name Leonides:

On Sept. 19th, at Three Gables, Swinly Dean, Aristide Leonides, beloved husband of Brenda Leonides, in his eighty-eighth year. Deeply regretted.

There was another announcement immediately below:

LEONIDES.—Suddenly, at his residence, Three Gables, Swinly Dean, Aristide Leonides. Deeply mourned by his loving children and grandchildren. Flowers to St. Eldred's Church, Swinly Dean.

I found the two announcements rather curious. There seemed to have been some faulty staff work resulting in overlapping. But my main preoccupation was Sophia. I hastily sent her a second telegram:

"Just seen news of your grandfather's death. Very sorry. Let me know when I can see you. Charles."

A telegram from Sophia reached me at six o'clock at my father's house. It said:

"Will be at Mario's nine o'clock. Sophia."

The thought of meeting Sophia again made me both nervous and excited. The time crept by with maddening slowness. I was at Mario's waiting twenty minutes too early. Sophia herself was only five minutes late.

It is always a shock to meet again someone whom you have not seen for a long time but who has been very much present in your mind during that period. When at last Sophia came through the swing doors our meeting seemed completely unreal. She was wearing black, and that, in some curious way, startled me. Most other women were wearing black, but I got it into my head that it was definitely mourning—and it surprised me that Sophia should be the kind of person who did wear black—even for a near relative.

We had cocktails—then went and found our table. We talked rather fast and feverishly—asking after old friends of the Cairo days. It was artificial conversation, but it tided us over the first awkwardness. I expressed commiseration for her grandfather's death and Sophia said quietly that it had been "very sudden." Then we started off again reminiscing. I began to feel, uneasily, that something was the matter —something, I mean, other than the first natural awkwardness of meeting again. There was something wrong, definitely wrong, with Sophia herself. Was she, perhaps, going to tell me that she had found some other man whom she cared for more than she did for me? That her feeling for me had been "all a mistake"?

Somehow I didn't think it was that—I didn't know what it was. Meanwhile we continued our artificial talk.

Then, quite suddenly, as the waiter placed coffee on the table and retired bowing, everything swung into focus. Here were Sophia and I sitting together as so often before at a small table in a restaurant. The years of our separation might never have been.

"*Sophia*," I said.

And immediately she said, "Charles!"

I drew a deep breath of relief.

"Thank goodness that's over," I said. "What's been the matter with us?"

"Probably my fault. I was stupid."

"But it's all right now?"

"Yes, it's all right now."

We smiled at each other.

"Darling!" I said. And then: "How soon will you marry me?"

Her smile died. The something, whatever it was, was back.

"I don't know," she said. "I'm not sure, Charles, that I can ever marry you."

"But, Sophia! Why not? Is it because you feel I'm a stranger? Do you want time to get used to me again? Is there someone else? No——" I broke off. "I'm a fool. It's none of those things."

"No, it isn't." She shook her head. I waited. She said in a low voice:

"It's my grandfather's death."

"Your grandfather's death? But why? What earthly differ-

9

ence can that make? You don't mean—surely you can't imagine—is it money? Hasn't he left any? But surely, dearest——"

"It isn't money." She gave a fleeting smile. "I think you'd be quite willing to 'take me in my shift,' as the old saying goes. And grandfather never lost any money in his life."

"Then what is it?"

"It's just his death—you see, I think, Charles, that he didn't just—die. I think he may have been— killed . . ."

I stared at her.

"But—what a fantastic idea. What made you think of it?"

"*I* didn't think of it. The doctor was queer to begin with. He wouldn't sign a certificate. They're going to have a post-mortem. It's quite clear that they suspect something is wrong."

I didn't dispute that with her. Sophia had plenty of brains; any conclusions she had drawn could be relied upon.

Instead I said earnestly:

"Their suspicions may be quite unjustified. But putting that aside, supposing that they are justified, how does that affect you and me?"

"It might under certain circumstances. You're in the Diplomatic Service. They're rather particular about wives. No —please don't say all the things that you're bursting to say. You're bound to say them—and I believe you really think them—and theoretically I quite agree with them. But I'm proud—I'm devilishly proud. I want our marriage to be a good thing for everyone—I don't want to represent one-half of a sacrifice for love! And, as I say, it *may* be all right . . ."

"You mean the doctor—may have made a mistake?"

"Even if he hasn't made a mistake, it won't matter—so long as the right person killed him."

"What *do* you mean, Sophia?"

"It was a beastly thing to say. But, after all, one might as well be honest."

She forestalled my next words.

"No, Charles, I'm not going to say any more. I've probably said too much already. But I was determined to come and meet you to-night—to see you myself and make you understand. We can't settle anything until this is cleared up."

"At least tell me about it."

10

She shook her head.

"I don't want to."

"But—Sophia——"

"No, Charles. I don't want you to see us from *my* angle. I want you to see us unbiased from the outside point of view."

"And how am I to do that?"

She looked at me, a queer light in her brilliant blue eyes.

"You'll get that from your father," she said.

I had told Sophia in Cairo that my father was Assistant Commissioner of Scotland Yard. He still held that office. At her words, I felt a cold weight settling down on me.

"It's as bad as that, then?"

"I think so. Do you see a man sitting at a table by the door all alone—rather a nice-looking stolid ex-Army type?"

"Yes."

"He was on Swinly Dean platform this evening when I got into the train."

"You mean he's followed you here?"

"Yes. I think we're all—how does one put it?—under observation. They more or less hinted that we'd all better not leave the house. But I was determined to see you." Her small square chin shot out pugnaciously. "I got out of the bathroom window and shinned down the water-pipe."

"Darling!"

"But the police are very efficient. And of course there was the telegram I sent you. Well—never mind—we're here—together . . . But from now on, we've both got to play a lone hand."

She paused and then added:

"Unfortunately—there's no doubt—about our loving each other."

"No doubt at all," I said. "And don't say unfortunately. You and I have survived a world war, we've had plenty of near escapes from sudden death—and I don't see why the sudden death of just one old man—how old was he, by the way?"

"Eighty-seven."

"Of course. It was in *The Times*. If you ask me, he just died of old age, and any self-respecting G.P. would accept the fact."

"If you'd known my grandfather," said Sophia, "you'd have been surprised at his dying of *anything*!"

III

I'D ALWAYS taken a certain amount of interest in my father's police work, but nothing had prepared me for the moment when I should come to take a direct and personal interest in it.

I had not yet seen the Old Man. He had been out when I arrived, and after a bath, a shave, and change I had gone out to meet Sophia. When I returned to the house, however, Glover told me that he was in his study.

He was at his desk, frowning over a lot of papers. He jumped up when I came in.

"Charles! Well, well, it's been a long time."

Our meeting, after five years of war, would have disappointed a Frenchman. Actually all the emotion of reunion was there all right. The Old Man and I are very fond of each other, and we understand each other pretty well.

"I've got some whisky," he said. "Say when. Sorry I was out when you got here. I'm up to the ears in work. Hell of a case just unfolding."

I leaned back in my chair and lit a cigarette.

"Aristide Leonides?" I asked.

His brows came down quickly over his eyes. He shot me a quick appraising glance. His voice was polite and steely.

"Now what makes you say that, Charles?"

"I'm right then?"

"How did you know about this?"

"Information received."

The Old Man waited.

"My information," I said, "came from the stable itself."

"Come on, Charles, let's have it."

"You mayn't like it," I said. "I met Sophia Leonides out in Cairo. I fell in love with her. I'm going to marry her. I met her to-night. She dined with me."

"Dined with you? In London? I wonder just how she managed to do that! The family was asked—oh, quite politely to stay put."

"Quite so. She shinned down a pipe from the bathroom window."

The Old Man's lips twitched for a moment into a smile.

"She seems," he said, "to be a young lady of some resource."

"But your police force is fully efficient," I said. "A nice Army type tracked her to Mario's. I shall figure in the reports you get. Five foot eleven, brown hair, brown eyes, dark-blue pin-stripe suit, etc."

The Old Man looked at me hard.

"Is this—serious?" he asked.

"Yes," I said. "It's serious, Dad."

There was a moment's silence.

"Do you mind?" I asked.

"I shouldn't have minded—a week ago. They're a well-established family—the girl will have money—and I know you. You don't lose your head easily. As it is——"

"Yes, Dad?"

"It may be all right, if——"

"If what?"

"If the right person did it."

It was the second time that night I had heard that phrase. I began to be interested.

"Just who *is* the right person?"

He threw a sharp glance at me.

"How much do you know about it all?"

"Nothing."

"Nothing?" He looked surprised. "Didn't the girl tell you?"

"No. She said she'd rather I saw it all—from an outside point of view."

"Now I wonder why that was?"

"Isn't it rather obvious?"

"No, Charles. I don't think it is."

He walked up and down frowning. He had lit a cigar and the cigar had gone out. That showed me just how disturbed the old boy was.

"How much do you know about the family?" he shot at me.

"Damn all! I know there was the old man and a lot of sons and grandchildren and in-laws. I haven't got the ramifications clear." I paused and then said, "You'd better put me in the picture, Dad."

"Yes." He sat down. "Very well then—I'll begin at the beginning—with Aristide Leonides. He arrived in England when he was twenty-four."

"A Greek from Smyrna."

13

"You do know that much?"

"Yes, but it's about all I do know."

The door opened and Glover came in to say that Chief-Inspector Taverner was here.

"He's in charge of the case," said my father. "We'd better have him in. He's been checking up on the family. Knows more about them than I do."

I asked if the local police had called in the Yard.

"It's in our jurisdiction. Swinly Dean is Greater London."

I nodded as Chief-Inspector Taverner came into the room. I knew Taverner from many years back. He greeted me warmly and congratulated me on my safe return.

"I'm putting Charles in the picture," said the Old Man. "Correct me if I go wrong, Taverner. Leonides came to London in 1884. He started up a little restaurant in Soho. It paid. He started up another. Soon he owned seven or eight of them. They all paid hand over fist."

"Never made any mistakes in anything he handled," said Chief-Inspector Taverner.

"He'd got a natural flair," said my father. "In the end he was behind most of the well-known restaurants in London. Then he went into the catering business in a big way."

"He was behind a lot of other businesses as well," said Taverner. "Second-hand clothes trade, cheap jewellery stores, lots of things. Of course," he added thoughtfully, "he was always a twister."

"You mean he was a crook?" I asked.

Taverner shook his head.

"No, I don't mean that. Crooked, yes—but not a crook. Never anything outside the law. But he was the sort of chap that thought up all the ways you can get round the law. He's cleaned up a packet that way even in this last war, and old as he was. Nothing he did was ever illegal—but as soon as he'd got on to it, you had to have a law about it, if you know what I mean. But by that time he'd gone on to the next thing."

"He doesn't sound a very attractive character," I said.

"Funnily enough, he was attractive. He'd got personality, you know. You could feel it. Nothing much to look at. Just a gnome—ugly little fellow—but magnetic—women always fell for him."

"He made a rather astonishing marriage," said my father. "Married the daughter of a country squire—an M.F.H."

14

I raised my eyebrows. "Money?"

The Old Man shook his head.

"No, it was a love match. She met him over some catering arrangements for a friend's wedding—and she fell for him. Her parents cut up rough, but she was determined to have him. I tell you, the man had charm—there was something exotic and dynamic about him that appealed to her. She was bored stiff with her own kind."

"And the marriage was happy?"

"It was very happy, oddly enough. Of course their respective friends didn't mix (those were the days before money swept aside all class distinctions) but that didn't seem to worry them. They did without friends. He built a rather preposterous house at Swinly Dean and they lived there and had eight children."

"This is indeed a family chronicle."

"Old Leonides was rather clever to choose Swinly Dean. It was only beginning to be fashionable then. The second and third golf courses hadn't been made. There was a mixture of Old Inhabitants who were passionately fond of their gardens and who liked Mrs. Leonides, and rich City men who wanted to be in with Leonides, so they could take their choice of acquaintances. They were perfectly happy, I believe, until she died of pneumonia in 1905."

"Leaving him with eight children?"

"One died in infancy. Two of the sons were killed in the last war. One daughter married and went to Australia and died there. An unmarried daughter was killed in a motor accident. Another died a year or two ago. There are two still living—the eldest son, Roger, who is married but has no children, and Philip, who married a well-known actress and has three children. Your Sophia, Eustace, and Josephine."

"And they are all living at—what is it?—Three Gables?"

"Yes. The Roger Leonides were bombed out early in the war. Philip and his family have lived there since 1937. And there's an elderly aunt, Miss de Haviland, sister of the first Mrs. Leonides. She always loathed her brother-in-law apparently, but when her sister died she considered it her duty to accept her brother-in-law's invitation to live with him and bring up the children."

"She's very hot on duty," said Inspector Taverner. "But she's not the kind that changes her mind about people. She always disapproved of Leonides and his methods——"

"Well," I said, "it seems a pretty good houseful. Who do you think killed him?"

Taverner shook his head.

"Early days," he said, "early days to say that."

"Come on, Taverner," I said. "I bet you think you know who did it. We're not in court, man."

"No," said Taverner gloomily. "And we may never be."

"You mean he may not have been murdered?"

"Oh, he was murdered all right. Poisoned. But you know what these poisoning cases are like. It's very tricky getting the evidence. Very tricky. All the possibilities may point one way——"

"That's what I'm trying to get at. You've got it all taped out in your mind, haven't you?"

"It's a case of very strong probability. It's one of those obvious things. The perfect set-up. But I don't know, I'm sure. It's tricky."

I looked appealingly at the Old Man.

He said slowly: "In murder cases, as you know, Charles, the obvious is usually the right solution. Old Leonides married again, ten years ago."

"When he was seventy-seven?"

"Yes, he married a young woman of twenty-four."

I whistled.

"What sort of a young woman?"

"A young woman out of a tea-shop. A perfectly respectable young woman—good-looking in an anæmic, apathetic sort of way."

"And she's the strong probability?"

"I ask you, sir," said Taverner. "She's only thirty-four now —and that's a dangerous age. She likes living soft. And there's a young man in the house. Tutor to the grandchildren. Not been in the war—got a bad heart or something. They're as thick as thieves."

I looked at him thoughtfully. It was, certainly, an old and familiar pattern. The mixture as before. And the second Mrs. Leonides was, my father had emphasised, very respectable. In the name of respectability many murders had been committed.

"What was it?" I asked. "Arsenic?"

"No. We haven't got the analyst's report yet—but the doctor thinks it's eserine."

"That's a little unusual, isn't it? Surely easy to trace the purchaser."

"Not this thing. It was his own stuff, you see. Eye-drops."

"Leonides suffered from diabetes," said my father. "He had regular injections of insulin. Insulin is given out in small bottles with a rubber cap. A hypodermic needle is pressed down through the rubber cap and the injection drawn up."

I guessed the next bit.

"And it wasn't insulin in the bottle, but eserine?"

"Exactly."

"And who gave him the injection?" I asked.

"His wife."

I understood now what Sophia meant by the "right person."

I asked: "Does the family get on well with the second Mrs. Leonides?"

"No. I gather they are hardly on speaking terms."

It all seemed clearer and clearer. Nevertheless, Inspector Taverner was clearly not happy about it.

"What don't you like about it?" I asked him.

"If she did it, Mr. Charles, it would have been so easy for her to substitute a bona fide bottle of insulin afterwards. In fact, if she is guilty, I can't imagine why on earth she didn't do just that."

"Yes, it does seem indicated. Plenty of insulin about?"

"Oh yes, full bottles and empty ones. And if she'd done that, ten to one the doctor wouldn't have spotted it. Very little is known of the post-mortem appearances in human poisoning by eserine. But as it was he checked up on the insulin (in case it was the wrong strength or something like that) and so, of course, he soon spotted that it *wasn't* insulin."

"So it seems," I said thoughtfully, "that Mrs. Leonides was either very stupid—or possibly very clever."

"You mean——"

"That she may be gambling on your coming to the conclusion that nobody could have been as stupid as she appears to have been. What are the alternatives? Any other—suspects?"

The Old Man said quietly:

"Practically anyone in the house could have done it. There was always a good store of insulin—at least a fortnight's supply. One of the phials could have been tampered with, and replaced in the knowledge that it would be used in due course."

"And anybody, more or less, had access to them?"

"They weren't locked away. They were kept on a special shelf in the medicine cupboard in the bathroom of his part of the house. Everybody in the house came and went freely."

"Any strong motive?"

My father sighed.

"My dear Charles, Aristide Leonides was enormously rich. He has made over a good deal of his money to his family, it is true, but it may be that somebody wanted more."

"But the one that wanted it most would be the present widow. Has her young man any money?"

"No. Poor as a church mouse."

Something clicked in my brain. I remembered Sophia's quotation. I suddenly remembered the whole verse of the nursery rhyme:

There was a crooked man and he went a crooked mile,
He found a crooked sixpence beside a crooked stile.
He had a crooked cat which caught a crooked mouse,
*   And they all lived together in a little crooked house.*

I said to Taverner:

"How does she strike you—Mrs. Leonides? What do you think of her?"

He replied slowly:

"It's hard to say—very hard to say. She's not easy. Very quiet—so you don't know what she's thinking. But she likes living soft—that I'll swear I'm right about. Puts me in mind, you know, of a cat, a big purring lazy cat . . . Not that I've anything against cats. Cats are all right . . ."

He sighed.

"What we want," he said, "is *evidence.*"

Yes, I thought, we *all* wanted evidence that Mrs. Leonides had poisoned her husband. Sophia wanted it, and I wanted it, and Chief-Inspector Taverner wanted it.

Then everything in the garden would be lovely!

But Sophia wasn't sure, and I wasn't sure, and I didn't think Chief-Inspector Taverner was sure either. . . .

IV

ON THE following day I went down to Three Gables with Taverner.

My position was a curious one. It was, to say the least of it, quite unorthodox. But the Old Man has never been highly orthodox.

I had a certain standing. I had worked with the Special Branch at the Yard during the early days of the war.

This, of course, was entirely different—but my earlier performances had given me, so to speak, a certain official standing.

My father said:

"If we're ever going to solve this case, we've got to get some inside dope. We've got to know all about the people in that house. We've got to know them from the *inside*—not the outside. You're the man who can get that for us."

I didn't like that. I threw my cigarette end into the grate as I said:

"I'm a police spy? Is that it? I'm to get the inside dope from Sophia whom I love and who both loves and trusts me, or so I believe."

The Old Man became quite irritable. He said sharply:

"For heaven's sake don't take the commonplace view. To begin with, you don't believe, do you, that your young woman murdered her grandfather?"

"Of course not. The idea's absolutely absurd."

"Very well—we don't think so either. She's been away for some years, she has always been on perfectly amicable terms with him. She has a very generous income and he would have been, I should say, delighted to hear of her engagement to you and would probably have made a handsome marriage settlement on her. We don't suspect her. Why should we? But you can make quite sure of one thing. If this thing isn't cleared up, that girl won't marry you. From what you've told me I'm fairly sure of that. And mark this, it's the kind of crime that may *never* be cleared up. We may be reasonably sure that the wife and her young man were in cahoots over it —but proving it will be another matter. There's not even ι case to put up to the D.P.P. so far. And unless we get

definite evidence against her, there'll always be a nasty doubt.
You see that, don't you?"

Yes, I saw that.

The Old Man then said quietly:

"Why not put it to her?"

"You mean—ask Sophia if I——" I stopped.

The Old Man was nodding his head vigorously.

"Yes, yes. I'm not asking you to worm your way in without telling the girl what you're up to. See what she has to say about it."

And so it came about that the following day I drove down with Chief-Inspector Taverner and Detective-Sergeant Lamb to Swinly Dean.

A little way beyond the golf course, we turned in at a gateway where I imagined that before the war there had been an imposing pair of gates. Patriotism or ruthless requisitioning had swept these away. We drove up a long curving drive flanked with rhododendrons and came out on a gravelled sweep in front of the house.

It was incredible! I wondered why it had been called *Three* Gables. Eleven Gables would have been more apposite! The curious thing was that it had a strange air of being distorted—and I thought I knew why. It was the type, really, of a cottage, it was a cottage swollen out of all proportion. It was like looking at a country cottage through a gigantic magnifying-glass. The slant-wise beams, the half-timbering, the gables—it was a little crooked house that had grown like a mushroom in the night!

Yet I got the idea. It was a Greek restaurateur's idea of something English. It was meant to be an Englishman's home —built the size of a castle! I wondered what the first Mrs. Leonides had thought of it. She had not, I fancied, been consulted or shown the plans. It was, most probably, her exotic husband's little surprise. I wondered if she had shuddered or smiled.

Apparently she had lived there quite happily.

"Bit overwhelming, isn't it?" said Inspector Taverner. "Of course, the old gentleman built on to it a good deal—making it into three separate houses, so to speak, with kitchens and everything. It's all tip-top inside, fitted up like a luxury hotel."

Sophia came out of the front door. She was hatless and wore a green shirt and a tweed skirt.

She stopped dead when she saw me.

"*You*?" she exclaimed.

I said:

"Sophia, I've got to talk to you. Where can we go?"

For a moment I thought she was going to demur, then she turned and said: "This way."

We walked down across the lawn. There was a fine view across Swinly Dean's No. 1 course—away to a clump of pine trees on a hill, and beyond it, to the dimness of hazy countryside.

Sophia led me to a rock-garden, now somewhat neglected, where there was a rustic wooden seat of great discomfort, and we sat down.

"Well?" she said.

Her voice was not encouraging.

I said my piece—all of it.

She listened very attentively. Her face gave little indication of what she was thinking, but when I came at last to a full stop, she sighed. It was a deep sigh.

"Your father," she said, "is a very clever man."

"The Old Man has his points. I think it's a rotten idea myself—but——"

She interrupted me.

"Oh no," she said. "It isn't a rotten idea at all. It's the only thing that might be any good. Your father, Charles, knows exactly what's been going on in my mind. He knows better than you do."

With sudden almost despairing vehemence, she drove one clenched hand into the palm of the other.

"I've *got* to have the truth. I've got to *know*."

"Because of us? But, dearest——"

"Not only because of us, Charles. I've got to know for my own peace of mind. You see, Charles, I didn't tell you last night—but the truth is—I'm afraid."

"Afraid?"

"Yes—afraid—afraid—afraid. The police think, your father thinks, you think, everybody thinks—that it was Brenda."

"The probabilities——"

"Oh yes, it's quite probable. It's possible. But when I say, 'Brenda probably did it,' I'm quite conscious that it's only wishful thinking. Because, you see, *I don't really think so*."

"You *don't* think so?" I said slowly.

21

"I don't *know*. You've heard about it all from the outside as I wanted you to. Now I'll show it you from the inside. I simply don't feel that Brenda is that kind of a person—she's not the sort of person, I feel, who would ever do anything that might involve her in any danger. She's far too careful of herself."

"How about this young man? Laurence Brown."

"Laurence is a complete rabbit. He wouldn't have the guts."

"I wonder."

"Yes, we don't really know, do we? I mean, people are capable of surprising one frightfully. One gets an idea of them into one's head, and sometimes it's absolutely wrong. Not always—but sometimes. But all the same, Brenda"—she shook her head—"she's always acted so completely in character. She's what I call the harem type. Likes sitting about and eating sweets and having nice clothes and jewellery and reading cheap novels and going to the cinema. And it's a queer thing to say, when one remembers that he was eighty-seven, but I really think she was rather thrilled by grandfather. He had a power, you know. I should imagine he could make a woman feel—oh—rather like a queen—the sultan's favourite! I think —I've always thought—that he made Brenda feel as though she were an exciting, romantic person. He's been clever with women all his life—and that kind of thing is a sort of art —you don't lose the knack of it, however old you are."

I left the problem of Brenda for the moment and harked back to a phrase of Sophia's which had disturbed me.

"Why did you say," I asked, "that you were afraid?"

Sophia shivered a little and pressed her hands together.

"Because it's true," she said in a low voice. "It's very important, Charles, that I should make you understand this. You see, we're a very queer family. . . . There's a lot of *ruthlessness* in us—and—different kinds of ruthlessness. That's what's so disturbing. The different kinds."

She must have seen incomprehension in my face. She went on, speaking energetically.

"I'll try and make what I mean clear. Grandfather, for instance. Once when he was telling us about his boyhood in Smyrna, he mentioned, quite casually, that he had stabbed two men. It was some kind of a brawl—there had been some unforgivable insult—I don't know—but it was just a thing that had happened quite naturally. He'd really practically forgotten about it. But it was, somehow, such a queer thing to hear about, quite casually, in *England*."

I nodded.

"That's one kind of ruthlessness," went on Sophia, "and then there was my grandmother. I only just remember her, but I've heard a good deal about her. I think she might have had the ruthlessness that comes from having no imagination whatever. All those fox-hunting forebears—and the old Generals, the shoot-'em-down type. Full of rectitude and arrogance, and not a bit afraid of taking responsibility in matters of life and death."

"Isn't that a bit far-fetched?"

"Yes, I dare say—but I'm always rather afraid of that type. It's full of rectitude but it *is* ruthless. And then there's my own mother—she's an actress—she's a darling, but she's got absolutely *no* sense of proportion. She's one of those unconscious egoists who can only see things in relation to how it affects *them*. That's rather frightening, sometimes, you know. And there's Clemency, Uncle Roger's wife. She's a scientist—she's doing some kind of very important research—she's ruthless too, in a kind of cold-blooded impersonal way. Uncle Roger's the exact opposite—he's the kindest and most lovable person in the world, but he's got a really terrific temper. Things make his blood boil and then he hardly knows what he's doing. And there's father——"

She made a long pause.

"Father," she said slowly, "is almost too well controlled. You never know what he's thinking. He never shows any emotion at all. It's probably a kind of unconscious self-defence against mother's absolute orgies of emotion, but sometimes—it worries me a little."

"My dear child," I said, "you're working yourself up unnecessarily. What it comes to in the end is that everybody, perhaps, is capable of murder."

"I suppose that's true. Even me."

"Not you!"

"Oh yes, Charles, you can't make me an exception. I suppose I *could* murder someone . . ." She was silent a moment or two, then added, "But if so, it would have to be for something really worth while!"

I laughed then. I couldn't help it. And Sophia smiled.

"Perhaps I'm a fool," she said, "but we've got to find

out the truth about grandfather's death. We've got to. If only i
was Brenda . . ."

I felt suddenly rather sorry for Brenda Leonides.

V

ALONG THE path towards us came a tall figure walking
briskly. It had on a battered old felt hat, a shapeless skirt, and
a rather cumbersome jersey.

"Aunt Edith," said Sophia.

The figure paused once or twice, stooping to the flower
borders, then it advanced upon us. I rose to my feet.

"This is Charles Hayward, Aunt Edith. My aunt, Miss
de Haviland."

Edith de Haviland was a woman of about seventy. She had
a mass of untidy grey hair, a weather-beaten face and a
shrewd and piercing glance.

"How d'ye do?" she said. "I've heard about you. Back
from the East. How's your father?"

Rather surprised, I said he was very well.

"Knew him when he was a boy," said Miss de Haviland.
"Knew his mother very well. You look rather like her. Have
you come to help us—or the other thing?"

"I hope to help," I said rather uncomfortably.

She nodded.

"We could do with some help. Place swarming with
policemen. Pop out at you all over the place. Don't like some
of the types. A boy who's been to a decent school oughtn't
to go into the police. Saw Moyra Kinoul's boy the other
day holding up the traffic at Marble Arch. Makes you feel
you don't know where you are!"

She turned to Sophia.

"Nannie's asking for you, Sophia. Fish."

"Bother," said Sophia. "I'll go and telephone about it."

She walked briskly towards the house. Miss de Haviland
turned and walked slowly in the same direction. I fell into
step beside her.

"Don't know what we'd all do without nannies," said
Miss de Haviland. "Nearly everybody's got an old nannie.
They come back and wash and iron and cook and do house-
work. Faithful. Chose this one myself—years ago."

She stopped and pulled viciously at an entangling twining bit of green.

"Hateful stuff—bindweed! Worst weed there is! Choking, entangling—and you can't get at it properly, runs along underground."

With her heel she ground the handful of greenstuff viciously underfoot.

"This is a bad business, Charles Hayward," she said. She was looking towards the house. "What do the police think about it? Suppose I mustn't ask you that. Seems odd to think of Aristide being poisoned. For that matter it seems odd to think of him being dead. I never liked him—never! But I can't get used to the idea of his being dead . . . Makes the house seem so—empty."

I said nothing. For all her curt way of speech, Edith de Haviland seemed in a reminiscent mood.

"Was thinking this morning—I've lived here a long time. Over forty years. Came here when my sister died. *He* asked me to. Seven children—and the youngest only a year old. . . . Couldn't leave 'em to be brought up by a dago, could I? An impossible marriage, of course. I always felt Marcia must have been—well—bewitched. Ugly common little foreigner! He gave me a free hand—I will say that. Nurses, governesses, school. And proper wholesome nursery food—not those queer spiced rice dishes *he* used to eat."

"And you've been here ever since?" I murmured.

"Yes. Queer in a way . . . I *could* have left, I suppose, when the children grew up and married . . . I suppose, really, I'd got interested in the garden. And then there was Philip. If a man marries an actress he can't expect to have any home life. Don't know why actresses have children. As soon as a baby's born they rush off and play in Repertory in Edinburgh or somewhere as remote as possible. Philip did the sensible thing—moved in here with his books."

"What does Philip Leonides do?"

"Writes books. Can't think why. Nobody wants to read them. All about obscure historical details. You've never even heard of them, have you?"

I admitted it.

"Too much money, that's what he's had," said Miss de Haviland. "Most people have to stop being cranks and earn a living."

"Don't his books pay?"

"Of course not. He's supposed to be a great authority on certain periods and all that. But he doesn't have to make his books pay—Aristide settled something like a hundred thousand pounds—something quite fantastic—on him! To avoid death duties! Aristide made them all financially independent. Roger runs Associated Catering—Sophia has a very handsome allowance. The children's money is in trust for them."

"So no one gains particularly by his death?"

She threw me a strange glance.

"Yes, they do. They all get more money. But they could probably have had it, if they asked for it, anyway."

"Have you any idea who poisoned him, Miss de Haviland?"

She replied characteristically:

"No, indeed I haven't. It's upset me very much. Not nice to think one has a Borgia sort of person loose about the house. I suppose the police will fasten on poor Brenda."

"You don't think they'll be right in doing so?"

"I simply can't tell. She's always seemed to me a singularly stupid and commonplace young woman—rather conventional. Not my idea of a poisoner. Still, after all, if a young woman of twenty-four marries a man close on eighty, it's fairly obvious that she's marrying him for his money. In the normal course of events she could have expected to become a rich widow fairly soon. But Artistide was a singularly tough old man. His diabetes wasn't getting any worse. He really looked like living to be a hundred. I suppose she got tired of waiting. . . ."

"In that case," I said, and stopped.

"In that case," said Miss de Haviland briskly, "it will be more or less all right. Annoying publicity, of course. But after all, she isn't one of the family."

"You've no other ideas?" I asked.

"What other ideas should I have?"

I wondered. I had a suspicion that there might be more going on under the battered felt hat than I knew.

Behind the perky, almost disconnected utterance, there was, I thought, a very shrewd brain at work. Just for a moment I even wondered whether Miss de Haviland had poisoned Aristide Leonides herself. . . .

It did not seem an impossible idea. At the back of my

mind was the way she had ground the bindweed into the soil with her heel with a kind of vindictive thoroughness.

I remembered the word Sophia had used. *Ruthlessness.*

I stole a sideways glance at Edith de Haviland.

Given good and sufficient reason . . . But what exactly would seem to Edith de Haviland good and sufficient reason?

To answer that, I should have to know her better.

VI

THE FRONT door was open. We passed through it into a rather surprisingly spacious hall. It was furnished with restraint —well-polished dark oak and gleaming brass. At the back, where the staircase would normally appear, was a white panelled wall with a door in it.

"My brother-in-law's part of the house," said Miss de Haviland. "The ground floor is Philip and Magda's."

We went through a doorway on the left into a large drawing-room. It had pale-blue panelled walls, furniture covered in heavy brocade, and on every available table and on the walls were hung photographs and pictures of actors, dancers, and stage scenes and designs. A Degas of ballet dancers hung over the mantelpiece. There were masses of flowers, enormous brown chrysanthemums and great vases of carnations.

"I suppose," said Miss de Haviland, "that you want to see Philip?"

Did I want to see Philip? I had no idea. All I had wanted to do was to see Sophia. That I had done. She had given emphatic encouragement to the Old Man's plan—but she had now receded from the scene and was presumably somewhere telephoning about fish, having given me no indication of how to proceed. Was I to approach Philip Leonides as a young man anxious to marry his daughter, or as a casual friend who had dropped in (surely not at such a moment!) or as an associate of the police?

Miss de Haviland gave me no time to consider her question. It was, indeed, not a question at all, but more an assertion. Miss de Haviland, I judged, was more inclined to assert than to question.

"We'll go to the library," she said.

She led me out of the drawing-room, along a corridor and in through another door.

It was a big room, full of books. The books did not confine themselves to the bookcases that reached up to the ceiling. They were on chairs and tables and even on the floor. And yet there was no sense of disarray about them.

The room was cold. There was some smell absent in it that I was conscious of having expected. It smelt of the mustiness of old books and just a little of beeswax. In a second or two I realised what I missed. It was the scent of tobacco. Philip Leonides was not a smoker.

He got up from behind his table as we entered—a tall man, aged somewhere around fifty, an extraordinarily handsome man. Everyone had laid so much emphasis on the ugliness of Aristide Leonides, that for some reason I expected his son to be ugly too. Certainly I was not prepared for this perfection of feature—the straight nose, the flawless line of jaw, the fair hair touched with grey that swept back from a well-shaped forehead.

"This is Charles Hayward, Philip," said Edith de Haviland.

"Ah, how do you do?"

I could not tell if he had ever heard of me. The hand he gave me was cold. His face was quite incurious. It made me rather nervous. He stood there, patient and uninterested.

"Where are those awful policemen?" demanded Miss de Haviland. "Have they been in here?"

"I believe Chief-Inspector"—(he glanced down at a card on the desk)—"er—Taverner is coming to talk to me presently."

"Where is he now?"

"I've no idea, Aunt Edith. Upstairs, I suppose."

"With Brenda?"

"I really don't know."

Looking at Philip Leonides, it seemed quite impossible that a murder could have been committed anywhere in his vicinity.

"Is Magda up yet?"

"I don't know. She's not usually up before eleven."

"That sounds like her," said Edith de Haviland.

What sounded like Mrs. Philip Leonides was a high voice talking very rapidly and approaching fast. The door behind me burst open and a woman came in. I don't know how she managed to give the impression of its being three women rather than one who entered.

She was smoking a cigarette in a long holder and was wearing a peach satin *négligé* which she was holding up with one hand. A cascade of Titian hair rippled down her back. Her face had that almost shocking air of nudity that a woman's has nowadays when it is not made up at all. Her eyes were blue and enormous and she was talking very rapidly in a husky rather attractive voice with a very clear enunciation.

"Darling, I can't stand it—I simply can't stand it—just think of the notices—it isn't in the papers yet, but of course it will be—and I simply can't make up my mind what I ought to wear at the inquest—very, very subdued—not black though, perhaps dark purple—and I simply haven't got a coupon left—I've lost the address of that dreadful man who sells them to me—you know, the garage somewhere near Shaftesbury Avenue—and if I went up there in the car the police would follow me, and they might ask the most awkward questions, mightn't they? I mean, what could one say? How calm you are, Philip! How can you be so calm? Don't you realise we can leave this awful house now? Freedom —freedom! Oh, how unkind—the poor old Sweetie—of course we'd never have left him while he was alive. He really did dote on us, didn't he—in spite of all the trouble that woman upstairs tried to make between us. I'm quite sure that if we had gone away and left him to her, he'd have cut us right out of everything. Horrible creature! After all, poor old Sweetie Pie was just on ninety—all the family feeling in the world couldn't have stood up against a dreadful woman who was on the spot. You know, Philip, I really believe that this would be a wonderful opportunity to put on the Edith Thompson play. This murder would give us a lot of advance publicity. Bildenstein said he could get the Thespian—that dreary play in verse about miners is coming off any minute—it's a wonderful part—wonderful. I know they say I must always play comedy because of my nose—but you know there's quite a lot of comedy to be got out of Edith Thompson—I don't think the author realised that— comedy always heightens the supense. I know just how I'd play it—commonplace, silly, make-believe up to the last minute and then——"

She cast out an arm—the cigarette fell out of the holder on to the polished mahogany of Philip's desk and began to burn it. Impassively he reached for it and dropped it into the wastepaper basket.

"And then," whispered Magda Leonides, her eyes suddenly widening, her face stiffening, "just *terror* . . ."

The stark fear stayed on her face for about twenty seconds, then her face relaxed, crumpled, a bewildered child was about to burst into tears.

Suddenly all emotion was wiped away as though by a sponge and, turning to me, she asked in a businesslike tone:

"Don't you think that would be the way to play Edith Thompson?"

I said I thought that would be exactly the way to play Edith Thompson. At the moment I could only remember very vaguely who Edith Thompson was, but I was anxious to start off well with Sophia's mother.

"Rather like Brenda, really, wasn't she?" said Magda. "D'you know, I never thought of that. It's very interesting. Shall I point that out to the inspector?"

The man behind the desk frowned very slightly.

"There's really no need, Magda," he said, "for you to see him at all. I can tell him anything he wants to know."

"Not see him?" Her voice went up. "But *of course* I must see him! Darling, darling, you're so terribly unimaginative! You don't realise the importance of *details*. He'll want to know exactly how and when everything happened, all the little things one noticed and wondered about at the time——"

"Mother," said Sophia, coming through the open door, "you're not to tell the inspector a lot of lies."

"Sophia—*darling* . . ."

"I know, precious, that you've got it all set and that you're ready to give a most beautiful performance. But you've got it wrong. Quite wrong."

"Nonsense. You don't know——"

"I do know. You've got to play it quite differently, darling. Subdued—saying very little—holding it all back—on your guard—protecting the family."

Magda Leonides' face showed the naïve perplexity of a child.

"Darling," she said, "do you really think——"

"Yes, I do. Throw it away. That's the idea."

Sophia added, as a little pleased smile began to show on her mother's face:

"I've made you some chocolate. It's in the drawing-room."

"Oh—good—I'm starving——"

She paused in the doorway.

"You don't know," she said, and the words appeared to be addressed either to me or to the bookshelf behind my head, "how lovely it is to have a daughter!"

On this exit line she went out.

"God knows," said Miss de Haviland, "what she will say to the police!"

"She'll be all right," said Sophia.

"She might say *anything*."

"Don't worry," said Sophia. "She'll play it the way the producer says. *I'm* the producer!"

She went out after her mother, then wheeled back to say:

"Here's Chief-Inspector Taverner to see you, Father. You don't mind if Charles stays, do you?"

I thought that a very faint air of bewilderment showed on Philip Leonides' face. It well might! But his incurious habit served me in good stead. He murmured:

"Oh certainly—certainly," in a rather vague voice.

Chief-Inspector Taverner came in, solid, dependable, and with an air of businesslike promptitude that was somehow soothing.

"Just a little unpleasantness," his manner seemed to say, "and then we shall be out of the house for good—and nobody will be more pleased than I shall. *We* don't want to hang about, I can assure you. . . ."

I don't know how he managed, without any words at all, but merely by drawing up a chair to the desk, to convey what he did, but it worked. I sat down unobtrusively a little way off.

"Yes, Chief-Inspector?" said Philip.

Miss de Haviland said abruptly:

"You don't want me, Chief-Inspector?"

"Not just at the moment, Miss de Haviland. Later, if I might have a few words with you——"

"Of course. I shall be upstairs."

She went out, shutting the door behind her.

"Well, Chief-Inspector?" Philip repeated.

"I know you're a very busy gentleman and I don't want to disturb you for long. But I may mention to you in confidence that our suspicions are confirmed. Your father did not die a natural death. His death was the result of an overdose of physostigmine—more usually known as eserine."

Philip bowed his head. He showed no particular emotion.

"I don't know whether that suggests anything to you?" Taverner went on.

"What should it suggest? My own view is that my father must have taken the poison by accident."

"You really think so, Mr. Leonides?"

"Yes, it seems to me perfectly possible. He was close on ninety, remember, and with very imperfect eyesight."

"So he emptied the contents of his eyedrop bottle into an insulin bottle. Does that really seem to you a credible suggestion, Mr. Leonides?"

Philip did not reply. His face became even more impassive.

Taverner went on:

"We have found the eyedrop bottle, empty—in the dustbin, with no fingerprints on it. That in itself is curious. In the normal way there should have been fingerprints. Certainly your father's, possibly his wife's, or the valet . . ."

Philip Leonides looked up.

"What about the valet?" he said. "What about Johnson?"

"You are suggesting Johnson as the possible criminal? He certainly had opportunity. But when we come to motive it is different. It was your father's custom to pay him a bonus every year—each year the bonus was increased. Your father made it clear to him that this was in lieu of any sum that he might otherwise have left him in his will. The bonus now, after seven years' service, has reached a very considerable sum every year and is still rising. It was obviously to Johnson's interest that your father should live as long as possible. Moreover, they were on excellent terms, and Johnson's record of past service is unimpeachable—he is a thoroughly skilled and faithful valet attendant." He paused. "We do not suspect Johnson."

Philip replied tonelessly: "I see."

"Now, Mr. Leonides, perhaps you will give me a detailed account of your own movements on the day of your father's death?"

"Certainly, Chief-Inspector. I was here, in this room, all that day—with the exception of meals, of course."

"Did you see your father at all?"

"I said good morning to him after breakfast as was my custom."

"Were you alone with him then?"

"My—er—stepmother was in the room."

"Did he seem quite as usual?"

With a slight hint of irony, Philip replied:

"He showed no foreknowledge that he was to be murdered that day."

"Is your father's portion of the house entirely separate from this?"

"Yes, the only access to it is through the door in the hall."

"Is that door kept locked?"

"No."

"Never?"

"I have never known it to be so."

"Anyone could go freely between that part of the house and this?"

"Certainly. It was only separate from the point of view of domestic convenience."

"How did you first hear of your father's death?"

"My brother Roger, who occupies the west wing of the floor above, came rushing down to tell me that my father had had a sudden seizure. He had difficulty in breathing and seemed very ill."

"What did you do?"

"I telephoned through to the doctor, which nobody seemed to have thought of doing. The doctor was out—but I left a message for him to come as soon as possible. I then went upstairs."

"And then?"

"My father was clearly very ill. He died before the doctor came."

There was no emotion in Philip's voice. It was a simple statement of fact.

"Where was the rest of your family?"

"My wife was in London. She returned shortly afterwards. Sophia was also absent, I believe. The two younger ones, Eustace and Josephine, were at home."

"I hope you won't misunderstand me, Mr. Leonides, if I ask you exactly how your father's death will affect your financial position."

"I quite appreciate that you want to know all the facts. My father made us financially independent a great many years ago. My brother he made Chairman and principal shareholder of Associated Catering—his largest company, and put the management of it entirely in his hands. He made over to me what he considered an equivalent sum—actually I think it was a hundred and fifty thousand pounds in various bonds and securities—so that I could use the capital as I chose. He also settled very generous amounts on my two sisters, who have since died."

"But he left himself still a very rich man?"

"No, actually he only retained for himself a comparatively modest income. He said it would give him an interest in life. Since that time"—for the first time a faint smile creased Philip's lips—"he has become, as the result of various undertakings, an even richer man that he was before."

"Your brother and yourself came here to live. That was not the result of any financial—difficulties?"

"Certainly not. It was a mere matter of convenience. My father always told us that we were welcome to make a home with him. For various domestic reasons this was a convenient thing for me to do.

"I was also," added Philip deliberately, "extremely fond of my father. I came here with my family in 1937. I pay no rent, but I pay my proportion of the rates."

"And your brother?"

"My brother came here as a result of the blitz, when his house in London was bombed in 1943."

"Now, Mr. Leonides, have you any idea what your father's testamentary dispositions are?"

"A very clear idea. He re-made his will in 1946. My father was not a secretive man. He had a great sense of family. He held a family conclave at which his solicitor was also present and who, at his request, made clear to us the terms of the will. These terms I expect you already know. Mr. Gaitskill will doubtless have informed you. Roughly, a sum of a hundred thousand pounds free of duty was left to my stepmother in addition to her already very generous marriage settlement. The residue of his property was divided into three portions, one to myself, one to my brother, and a third in trust for the three grandchildren. The estate is a large one, but the death duties, of course, will be very heavy."

"Any bequests to servants or to charity?"

"No bequests of any kind. The wages paid to servants were increased annually if they remained in his service."

"You are not—you will excuse my asking—in actual need of money, Mr. Leonides?"

"Income tax, as you know, is somewhat heavy, Chief-Inspector—but my income amply suffices for my needs—and for my wife's. Moreover, my father frequently made us all very generous gifts, and had any emergency arisen, he would have come to the rescue immediately."

Philip added coldly and clearly:

"I can assure you that I had no financial reason for desiring my father's death, Chief-Inspector."

"I am very sorry, Mr. Leonides, if you think I suggested anything of the kind. But we have to get at all the facts. Now I'm afraid I must ask you some rather delicate questions. They refer to the relations between your father and his wife. Were they on happy terms together?"

"As far as I know, perfectly."

"No quarrels?"

"I do not think so."

"There was a—great disparity in age?"

"There was."

"Did you—excuse me—approve of your father's second marriage."

"My approval was not asked."

"That is not an answer, Mr. Leonides."

"Since you press the point, I will say that I considered the marriage unwise."

"Did you remonstrate with your father about it."

"When I heard of it, it was an accomplished fact."

"Rather a shock to you—eh?"

Philip did not reply.

"Was there any bad feeling about the matter?"

"My father was at perfect liberty to do as he pleased."

"Your relations with Mrs. Leonides have been amicable?"

"Perfectly."

"You are on friendly terms with her?"

"We very seldom meet."

Chief-Inspector Taverner shifted his ground.

"Can you tell me something about Mr. Laurence Brown?"

"I'm afraid I can't. He was engaged by my father."

"But he was engaged to teach your children, Mr. Leonides."

"True. My son was a sufferer from infantile paralysis

—fortunately a light case—and it was considered not advisable to send him to a public school. My father suggested that he and my young daughter Josephine should have a private tutor—the choice at the time was rather limited—since the tutor in question must be ineligible for military service. This young man's credentials were satisfactory, my father and my aunt (who has always looked after the children's welfare) were satisfied, and I acquiesced. I may add that I have no fault to find with his teaching, which has been conscientious and adequate."

"His living quarters are in your father's part of the house, not here?"

"There was more room up there."

"Have you ever noticed—I am sorry to ask this—any signs of intimacy between Laurence Brown and your stepmother?"

"I have had no opportunuity of observing anything of the kind."

"Have you heard any gossip or tittle-tattle on the subject?"

"I don't listen to gossip or tittle-tattle, Chief-Inspector."

"Very creditable," said Inspector Taverner. "So you've seen no evil, heard no evil, and aren't speaking any evil?"

"If you like to put it that way, Chief-Inspector."

Inspector Taverner got up.

"Well," he said, "thank you very much, Mr. Leonides."

I followed him unobtrusively out of the room.

"Whew," said Taverner, "he's a cold fish!"

VII

"AND NOW," said Taverner, "we'll go and have a word with Mrs. Philip. Magda West, her stage name is."

"Is she any good?" I asked. "I know her name, and I believe I've seen her in various shows, but I can't remember when and where."

"She's one of those Near Successes," said Taverner. "She's starred once or twice in the West End, she's made quite a name for herself in Repertory—she plays a lot for the little highbrow theatres and the Sunday clubs. The truth is, I think, she's been handicapped by not having to earn her living at it. She's been able to pick and choose, and to go where she likes and occasionally to put up the money and finance a show where she's fancied a certain part—usually the last part in the world to suit her. Result is, she's receded a bit into the amateur class rather than the professional. She's good, mind you, especially in comedy—but managers don't like her much —they say she's too independent, and she's a trouble-maker—foments rows and enjoys a bit of mischief-making. I don't know how much of it is true—but she's not too popular amongst her fellow artists."

Sophia came out of the drawing-room and said: "My mother is in here, Chief-Inspector."

I followed Taverner into the big drawing-room. For a moment I hardly recognised the woman who sat on the brocaded settee.

The titian hair was piled high on her head in an Edwardian coiffure, and she was dressed in a well-cut dark-grey coat and skirt with a delicately pleated pale mauve shirt fastened at the neck by a small cameo brooch. For the first time I was aware of the charm of her delightfully tip-tilted nose. I was faintly reminded of Athene Seyler—and it seemed quite impossible to believe that this was the tempestuous creature in the peach *négligé*.

"Inspector Taverner?" she said. "*Do* come in and sit down. Will you smoke? This is a most terrible business. I simply feel at the moment that I just can't take it in."

Her voice was low and emotionless, the voice of a person determined at all costs to display self-control. She went on:

"Please tell me if I can help you in any way."

"Thank you, Mrs. Leonides. Where were you at the time of the tragedy?"

"I suppose I must have been driving down from London. I'd lunched that day at the Ivy with a friend. Then we'd gone to a dress show. We had a drink with some other friends at the Berkeley. Then I started home. When I got here everything was in commotion. It seemed my father-in-law had had a sudden seizure. He was—dead." Her voice trembled just a little.

"You were fond of your father-in-law?"

"I was devoted——"

Her voice rose. Sophia adjusted, very slightly, the angle of the Degas picture. Magda's voice dropped to its former subdued tone.

"I was very fond of him," she said in a quiet voice. "We all were. He was—very good to us."

"Did you get on well with Mrs. Leonides?"

"We didn't see very much of Brenda."

"Why was that?"

"Well, we hadn't much in common. Poor dear Brenda. Life must have been hard for her sometimes."

Again Sophia fiddled with the Degas.

"Indeed? In what way?"

"Oh, I don't know." Magda shook her head, with a sad little smile.

"Was Mrs. Leonides happy with her husband?"

"Oh, I think so."

"No quarrels?"

Again the slight smiling shake of the head.

"I really don't know, Inspector. Their part of the house is quite separate."

"She and Mr. Laurence Brown were very friendly, were they not?"

Magda Leonides stiffened. Her eyes opened reproachfully at Taverner.

"I don't think," she said with dignity, "that you ought to ask me things like that. Brenda was quite friendly to *everyone*. She is really a very amiable sort of person."

"Do you like Mr. Laurence Brown?"

"He's very quiet. Quite nice, but you hardly know he's there. I haven't really seen very much of him."

"Is his teaching satisfactory?"

"I suppose so. I really wouldn't know. Philip seems quite satisfied."

Taverner essayed some shock tactics.

"I'm sorry to ask you this, but in your opinion was there anything in the nature of a love affair between Mr. Brown and Mrs. Brenda Leonides?"

Magda got up. She was very much the *grande dame*.

"I have never seen any evidence of anything of that kind," she said, "I don't think really, Inspector, that that is a question you ought to ask me. She was my father-in-law's wife."

I almost applauded.

The Chief-Inspector also rose.

"More a question for the servants?" he suggested.

Magda did not answer.

38

"Thank you, Mrs. Leonides," said the Inspector and went out.

"You did that beautifully, darling," said Sophia to her mother warmly.

Magda twisted up a curl reflectively behind her right ear and looked at herself in the glass.

"Ye-es," she said, "I *think* it was the right way to play it."

Sophia looked at me.

"Oughtn't you," she asked, "to go with the Inspector?"

"Look here, Sophia, what am I supposed——"

I stopped. I could not very well ask outright in front of Sophia's mother exactly what my role was supposed to be. Magda Leonides had so far evinced no interest in my presence at all, except as a useful recipient of an exit line on daughters. I might be a reporter, her daughter's fiancé, or an obscure hanger-on of the police force, or even an undertaker—to Magda Leonides they would, one and all come under the general heading of audience.

Looking down at her feet, Mrs. Leonides said with dissatisfaction:

"These shoes are wrong. Frivolous."

Obeying Sophia's imperious wave of the head, I hurried after Taverner. I caught him up in the outer hall just going through the door to the stairway.

"Just going up to see the elder brother," he explained.

I put my problem to him without more ado.

"Look here, Taverner, who am I supposed to *be*?"

He looked surprised.

"Who are you supposed to be?"

"Yes, what am I doing here in this house? If anyone asks me, what do I say?"

"Oh I see." He considered a moment. Then he smiled. "Has anybody asked you?"

"Well—no."

"Then why not leave it at that. *Never explain.* That's a very good motto. Especially in a house upset like this house is. Everyone is far too full of their own private worries and fears to be in a questioning mood. They'll take you for granted so long as you just seem sure of yourself. It's a great mistake ever to say anything when you needn't. H'm, now we go through this door and up the stairs. Nothing locked. Of course you realise, I expect, that these questions I'm asking

39

are all a lot of hooey! Doesn't matter a hoot who was in the house and who wasn't, or where they all were on that particular day——"

"Then why——"

He went on; "Because it at least gives me a chance to look at them all, and size them up, and hear what they've got to say, and to hope that, quite by chance, somebody might give me a useful pointer." He was silent a moment and then murmured: "I bet Mrs. Magda Leonides could spill a mouthful if she chose."

"Would it be reliable?" I asked.

"Oh no," said Taverner, "it wouldn't be reliable. But it might start a possible line of inquiry. Everybody in the damned house had means and opportunity. What I want is a motive."

At the top of the stairs, a door barred off the right-hand corridor. There was a brass knocker on it and Inspector Taverner duly knocked.

It was opened with startling suddenness by a man who must have been standing just inside. He was a clumsy giant of a man, with powerful shoulders, dark rumpled hair, and an exceedingly ugly but at the same time rather pleasant face. His eyes looked at us and then quickly away in that furtive, embarrassed manner which shy but honest people often adopt.

"Oh, I say," he said. "Come in. Yes, do. I was going—but it doesn't matter. Come into the sitting-room. I'll get Clemency—oh, you're there, darling. It's Chief-Inspector Taverner. He—are there any cigarettes? Just wait a minute. If you don't mind." He collided with a screen, said "I beg your pardon" to it in a flustered manner, and went out of the room.

It was rather like the exit of a bumble-bee and left a noticeable silence behind it.

Mrs. Roger Leonides was standing up by the window. I was intrigued at once by her personality and by the atmosphere of the room in which we stood.

The walls were painted white—really white, not an ivory or a pale cream which is what one usually means when one says "white" in house decoration. They had no pictures on them except one over the mantelpiece, a geometrical fantasia in triangles of dark grey and battleship blue. There was hardly any furniture—only mere utilitarian necessities, three or four chairs, a glass-topped table, one small bookshelf. There were no ornaments. There was light and space and air. It was as different from the big brocaded and flowered drawing-room on the floor below as chalk from cheese. And Mrs. Roger Leonides was as different from Mrs. Philip Leonides as one woman could be from another. Whilst one felt that Magda Leonides could be, and often was, at least half a dozen different women, Clemency Leonides, I was sure, could never be anyone but herself. She was a woman of very sharp and definite personality.

She was about fifty, I suppose; her hair was grey, cut very short in what was almost an Eton crop but which grew so beautifully on her small well-shaped head that it had none of the ugliness I have always associated with that particular cut. She had an intelligent, sensitive face, with light-grey eyes of a peculiar and searching intensity. She had on a simple dark-red woollen frock that fitted her slenderness perfectly.

She was, I felt at once, rather an alarming woman . . . I think, because I judged that the standards by which she lived might not be those of an ordinary woman. I understood at once why Sophia had used the word ruthlessness in connection with her. The room was cold and I shivered a little.

Clemency Leonides said in a quiet, well-bred voice:

"Do sit down, Chief-Inspector. Is there any further news?"

"Death was due to eserine, Mrs. Leonides."

She said thoughtfully:

"So that makes it murder. It couldn't have been an accident of any kind, could it?"

"No, Mrs. Leonides."

"Please be very gentle with my husband, Chief-Inspector. This will affect him very much. He worshipped his father and he feels things very acutely. He is an emotional person."

"You were on good terms with your father-in-law, Mrs. Leonides?"

"Yes, on quite good terms." She added quietly: "I did not like him very much."

"Why was that?"

"I disliked his objectives in life—and his methods of attaining them."

"And Mrs. Brenda Leonides?"

"Brenda? I never saw very much of her."

"Do you think it possible that there was anything between her and Mr. Laurence Brown?"

"You mean—some kind of a love affair? I shouldn't think so. But I really wouldn't know anything about it."

Her voice sounded completely uninterested.

Roger Leonides came back with a rush, and the same bumble-bee effect.

"I got held up," he said. "Telephone. Well, Inspector? Well? Have you got news? What caused my father's death?"

"Death was due to eserine poisoning."

"It was? My God! Then it was that woman! She couldn't wait! He took her more or less out of the gutter and this is his reward. She murdered him in cold blood! God, it makes my blood boil to think of it."

"Have you any particular reason for thinking that?" Taverner asked.

Roger was pacing up and down, tugging at his hair with both hands.

"Reason? Why, who else could it be? I've never trusted her—never liked her! We've none of us liked her. Philip and I were both appalled when Dad came home one day and told us what he had done! At his age! It was madness —*madness*. My father was an amazing man, Inspector. In intellect he was as young and fresh as a man of forty. Everything I have in the world I owe to him. He did everything for me— never failed me. It was I who failed *him*—when I think of it——"

He dropped heavily on to a chair. His wife came quietly to his side.

"Now, Roger, that's enough. Don't work yourself up."

"I know, dearest—I know," he took her hand. "But how can I keep calm—how can I help feeling——"

"But we must all keep calm, Roger. Chief-Inspector Taverner wants our help."

"That is right, Mrs. Leonides."

Roger cried:

"Do you know what I'd like to do? I'd like to strangle that woman with my own hands. Grudging that dear old man a few extra years of life. If I had her here——" He sprang up. He was shaking with rage. He held out convulsive hands. "Yes, I'd wring her neck, wring her neck . . ."

"Roger!" said Clemency sharply.

He looked at her, abashed.

"Sorry, dearest." He turned to us. "I do apologise. My feelings get the better of me. I—excuse me——"

He went out of the room again. Clemency Leonides said with a very faint smile:

"Really, you know, he wouldn't hurt a fly."

Taverner accepted her remark politely.

Then he started on his so-called routine questions. Clemency Leonides replied concisely and accurately.

Roger Leonides had been in London on the day of his father's death at Box House, the headquarters of the Associated Catering. He had returned early in the afternoon and had spent some time with his father as was his custom. She herself had been, as usual, at the Lambert Institute in Gower Street where she worked. She had returned to the house just before six o'clock.

"Did you see your father-in-law?"

"No. The last time I saw him was on the day before. We had coffee with him after dinner."

"But you did not see him on the day of his death?"

"No. I actually went over to his part of the house because Roger thought he had left his pipe there—a very precious pipe, but as it happened he had left it on the hall table there, so I did not need to disturb the old man. He often dozed off about six."

"When did you hear of his illness?"

"Brenda came rushing over. That was just a minute or two after half-past six."

These questions, as I knew, were unimportant, but I was aware how keen was Inspector Taverner's scrutiny of the woman who answered them. He asked her a few questions about the nature of her work in London. She said that it had to do with the radiation effects of atomic disintegration.

"You work on the atom bomb, in fact?"

"The work has nothing destructive about it. The Institute is carrying out experiments on the therapeutic effects."

When Taverner got up, he expressed a wish to look round their part of the house. She seemed a little surprised, but showed him its extent readily enough. The bedroom with its twin beds and white coverlets and its simplified toilet appliances reminded me again of a hospital or some monastic cell. The bathroom, too, was severely plain with no special luxury fitting and no array of cosmetics. The kitchen was bare, spotlessly clean, and well equipped with labour-saving devices of a practical kind. Then we came to a door which Clemency opened, saying: "This is my husband's special room."

"Come in," said Roger. "Come in."

I drew a faint breath of relief. Something in the spotless austerity elsewhere had been getting me down. This was an intensely personal room. There was a large roll-top desk untidily covered with papers, old pipes, and tobacco ash. There were big shabby easy-chairs. Persian rugs covered the floor. On the walls were groups, their photography somewhat faded. School groups, cricket groups, military groups. Water-colour sketches of deserts and minarets, and of sailing-boats and sea effects and sunsets. It was, somehow, a pleasant room, the room of a lovable, friendly, companionable man.

Roger, clumsily, was pouring out drinks from a tantalus, sweeping books and papers off one of the chairs.

"Place is in a mess. I was turning out. Clearing up old papers. Say when." The inspector declined a drink. I accepted.

"You must forgive me just now," went on Roger. He brought my drink over to me, turning his head to speak to Taverner as he did so. "My feelings ran away with me."

He looked round almost guiltily, but Clemency Leonides had not accompanied us into the room.

"She's so wonderful," he said. "My wife, I mean. All through this, she's been splendid—*splendid*! I can't tell you how I admire that woman. And she's had such a hard time—a terrible time. I'd like to tell you about it. Before we were married, I mean. Her first husband was a fine chap—fine mind, I mean—but terribly delicate—tubercular as a matter of fact. He was doing very valuable research work on crystallography, I believe. Poorly paid and very exacting, but he wouldn't give up. She slaved for him, practically kept him, knowing all the time that he was dying. And never a complaint—never a murmur of weariness. She always said she was happy. Then he died, and she was terribly cut up. At last she agreed to marry me. I was so glad to be able to give her some rest, some happiness, I wished she would stop working, but of course she felt it her duty in war time, and she still seems to feel she should go on. But she's

44

een a wonderful wife—the most wonderful wife a man ever
ad. Gosh, I've been lucky! I'd do anything for her."

Taverner made a suitable rejoinder. Then he embarked
nce more on the familiar routine questions. When had he
irst heard of his father's illness?

"Brenda had rushed over to call me. My father was
ll—she said he had had a seizure of some sort.

"I'd been sitting with the dear old boy only about half an
our earlier. He'd been perfectly all right then. I rushed
ver. He was blue in the face, gasping. I dashed down to
hilip. He rang up the doctor. I—we couldn't do anything.
Of course I never dreamed for a moment then that there had
een any funny business. Funny? Did I say funny? God, what
a word to use."

With a little difficulty, Taverner and I disentangled our-
elves from the emotional atmosphere of Roger Leonides'
oom and found ourselves outside the door, once more at the
op of the stairs.

"Whew!" said Taverner. "What a contrast from the other
rother." He added, rather inconsequently: "Curious things,
ooms. Tell you quite a lot about the people who live in
hem."

I agreed and he went on:

"Curious the people who marry each other, too, isn't it?"

I was not quite sure if he was referring to Clemency and
Roger, or to Philip and Magda. His words applied equally
well to either. Yet it seemed to me that both the marriages
might be classed as happy ones. Roger's and Clemency's
certainly was.

"I shouldn't say he was a poisoner, would you?" asked
Taverner. "Not off-hand, I wouldn't. Of course you never
know. Now she's more the type. Remorseless sort of woman.
Might be a bit mad."

Again I agreed. "But I don't suppose," I said, "that
she'd murder anyone just because she didn't approve of their
aims and mode of life. Perhaps, if she really hated the old
man—but are any murders committed just out of pure hate?"

"Precious few," said Taverner. "I've never come across
one myself. No, I think we're a good deal safer to stick
o Mrs. Brenda. But God knows if we'll ever get any
vidence."

VIII

A PARLOURMAID opened the door of the opposite wing to us. She looked scared but slightly contemptuous when she saw Taverner.

"You want to see the mistress?"

"Yes, please."

She showed us into a big drawing-room and went out.

Its proportions were the same as the drawing-room on the ground floor below. There were coloured cretonnes, very gay in colour, and striped silk curtains. Over the mantelpiece was a portrait that held my gaze riveted—not only because of the master hand that had painted it, but also because of the arresting face of the subject.

It was the portrait of a little old man with dark, piercing eyes. He wore a black velvet skull cap and his head was sunk down in his shoulders, but the vitality and power of the man radiated forth from the canvas. The twinkling eyes seemed to hold mine.

"That's him," said Chief-Inspector Taverner ungrammatically. "Painted by Augustus John. Got a personality, hasn't he?"

"Yes," I said, and felt the monosyllable was inadequate.

I understood now just what Edith de Haviland had meant when she said the house seemed so empty without him. This was the Original Crooked Little Man who had built the Crooked Little House—and without him the Crooked Little House had lost its meaning.

"That's his first wife over there, painted by Sargent," said Taverner.

I examined the picture on the wall between the windows. It had a certain cruelty like many of Sargent's portraits. The length of the face was exaggerated, I thought—so was the faint suggestion of horsiness—the indisputable correctness. It was a portrait of a typical English Lady—in Country (not Smart) Society. Handsome, but rather lifeless. A most unlikely wife for the grinning, powerful little despot over the mantelpiece.

The door opened and Sergeant Lamb stepped in.

"I've done what I could with the servants, sir," he said. "Didn't get anything."

46

Taverner sighed.

Sergeant Lamb took out his notebook and retreated to the far end of the room, where he seated himself unobtrusively.

The door opened again and Aristide Leonides' second wife came into the room.

She wore black—very expensive black and a good deal of it. It swathed her up to the neck and down to the wrists. She moved easily and indolently, and black certainly suited her. Her face was mildly pretty, and she had rather nice brown hair arranged in somewhat too elaborate style. Her face was well powdered and she had on lipstick and rouge, but she had clearly been crying. She was wearing a string of very large pearls and she had a big emerald ring on one hand and an enormous ruby on the other.

There was one other thing I noticed about her. She looked frightened.

"Good morning, Mrs. Leonides," said Taverner easily. "I'm sorry to have to trouble you again."

She said in a flat voice:

"I suppose it can't be helped."

"You understand, don't you, Mrs. Leonides, that if you wish your solicitor to be present, that is perfectly in order?"

I wondered if she did understand the significance of those words. Apparently not. She merely said rather sulkily:

"I don't like Mr. Gaitskill. I don't want him."

"You could have your own solicitor, Mrs. Leonides."

"Must I? I don't like solicitors. They confuse me."

"It's entirely for you to decide," said Taverner, producing an automatic smile. "Shall we go on, then?"

Sergeant Lamb licked his pencil. Brenda Leonides sat down on a sofa facing Taverner.

"Have you found out anything?" she asked.

I noticed her fingers nervously twisting and untwisting a pleat of the chiffon of her dress.

"We can state definitely now that your husband died as a result of eserine poisoning."

"You mean those eyedrops killed him?"

"It seems quite certain that when you gave Mr. Leonides that last injection, it was eserine that you injected and not insulin."

"But I didn't know that. I didn't have anything to do with it. Really I didn't, Inspector."

47

"Then somebody must have deliberately replaced the insulin by the eyedrops."

"What a wicked thing to do!"

"Yes, Mrs. Leonides."

"Do you think—someone did it on purpose? Or by accident? It couldn't have been a—a joke, could it?"

Taverner said smoothly:

"We don't think it was a joke, Mrs. Leonides."

"It must have been one of the servants."

Taverner did not answer.

"It must. I don't see who else could have done it."

"Are you sure? Think, Mrs. Leonides. Haven't you any ideas at all? There's been no ill-feeling anywhere? No quarrel? No grudge?"

She still stared at him with large defiant eyes.

"I've no idea at all," she said.

"You had been at the cinema that afternoon, you said?"

"Yes—I came in at half-past six—it was time for the insulin—I—I—gave him the injection just the same as usual and then he—he went all queer. I was terrified—I rushed over to Roger—I've told you all this before. Have I got to go over it again and again?" Her voice rose hysterically.

"I'm sorry, Mrs. Leonides. Now can I speak to Mr. Brown?"

"To Laurence? Why? He doesn't know anything about it."

"I'd like to speak to him all the same."

She stared at him suspiciously.

"Eustace is doing Latin with him in the schoolroom. Do you want him to come here?"

"No—we'll go to him."

Taverner went quickly out of the room. The sergeant and I followed.

"You've put the wind up her, sir," said Sergeant Lamb.

Taverner grunted. He led the way up a short flight of steps and along a passage into a big room looking over the garden. There a fair-haired young man of about thirty and a handsome, dark boy of sixteen were sitting at a table.

They looked up at our entrance. Sophia's brother Eustace looked at me, Laurence Brown fixed an agonised gaze on Chief-Inspector Taverner.

I have never seen a man look so completely paralysed with

fright. He stood up, then sat down again. He said, and his voice was almost a squeak:

"Oh—er—good morning, Inspector."

"Good morning," Taverner was curt. "Can I have a word with you?"

"Yes, of course. Only too pleased. At least——"

Eustace got up.

"Do you want me to go away, Chief-Inspector?" His voice was pleasant with a faintly arrogant note.

"We—we can continue our studies later," said the tutor.

Eustace strolled negligently towards the door. He walked rather stiffly. Just as he went through the door he caught my eye, drew a forefinger across the front of his throat and grinned. Then he shut the door behind him.

"Well, Mr. Brown," said Taverner. "The analysis is quite definite. It was eserine that cause Mr. Leonides' death."

"I—you mean—Mr. Leonides was really poisoned? I have been hoping——"

"He was poisoned," said Taverner curtly. "Someone substituted eserine eyedrops for insulin."

"I can't believe it . . . It's incredible."

"The question is, who had a motive?"

"Nobody. Nobody at all!" The young man's voice rose excitedly.

"You wouldn't like to have your solicitor present, would you?" inquired Taverner.

"I haven't got a solicitor. I don't want one. I have nothing to hide—nothing . . ."

"And you quite understand that what you say is about to be taken down?"

"I'm innocent—I assure you, I'm innocent."

"I have not suggested anything else." Taverner paused. "Mrs. Leonides was a good deal younger than her husband, was she not?"

"I—I suppose so—I mean, well, yes."

"She must have felt lonely sometimes?"

Laurence Brown did not answer. He passed his tongue over his dry lips.

"To have a companion of more or less her own age living here must have been agreeable to her?"

"I—no, not at all—I mean—I don't know."

49

"It seems to me quite natural that an attachment should have sprung up between you."

The young man protested vehemently.

"It didn't! It wasn't! Nothing of the kind! I know what you're thinking, but it wasn't so! Mrs. Leonides was very kind to me always and I had the greatest—the greatest respect for her—but nothing more—nothing more, I do assure you. It's monstrous to suggest things of that kind! Monstrous! I wouldn't kill *anybody*—or tamper with bottles—or anything like that. I'm very sensitive and highly strung. I—the very idea of killing is a *nightmare* to me—they quite understood that at the tribunal—I have religious objections to killing. I did hospital work instead—stoking boilers—terribly heavy work —I couldn't go on with it—but they let me take up educational work. I have done my best here with Eustace and with Josephine—a very intelligent child, but difficult. And everybody has been most kind to me—Mr. Leonides and Mrs. Leonides and Miss de Haviland. And now this awful thing happens . . . And you suspect me—*me*—of murder!"

Inspector Taverner looked at him with a slow, appraising interest.

"I haven't said so," he remarked.

"But you think so! I know you think so! They all think so! They look at me. I—I can't go on talking to you. I'm not well."

He hurried out of the room. Taverner turned his head slowly to look at me.

"Well, what do you think of him?"

"He's scared stiff."

"Yes, I know, but is he a murderer?"

"If you ask me," said Sergeant Lamb, "he'd never have had the nerve."

"He'd never have bashed anyone on the head, or shot off a pistol," agreed the Chief-Inspector. "But in this particular crime what is there to do? Just monkey about with a couple of bottles. . . . Just help a very old man out of the world in a comparatively painless manner."

"Practically euthanasia," said the sergeant.

"And then, perhaps, after a decent interval, marriage with a woman who inherits a hundred thousand pounds free of legacy duty, who already has about the same amount settled upon her, and who has in addition pearls and rubies and emeralds the size of what's-its-name eggs!"

"Ah, well——" Taverner sighed. "It's all theory and conjecture! I managed to scare him all right, but that doesn't prove anything. He's just as likely to be scared if he's innocent. And anyway, I rather doubt if he *was* the one actually to do it. More likely to have been the woman—only why on earth didn't she throw away the insulin bottle, or rinse it out?" He turned to the sergeant. "No evidence from the servants about any goings on?"

"The parlourmaid says they're sweet on each other."

"What grounds?"

"The way he looks at her when she pours out his coffee."

"Fat lot of good that would be in a court of law! Definitely no carryings on?"

"Not that anybody's seen."

"I bet they would have seen, too, if there had been anything to see. You know I'm beginning to believe there really is nothing between them." He looked at me. "Go back and talk to her. I'd like your impression of her."

I went, half-reluctantly, yet I was interested.

IX

I FOUND Brenda Leonides sitting exactly where I had left her. She looked up sharply as I entered.

"Where's Inspector Taverner? Is he coming back?"

"Not just yet."

"Who are you?"

At last I had been asked the question that I had been expecting all the morning.

I answered it with reasonable truth.

"I'm connected with the police, but I'm also a friend of the family."

"The family! Beasts! I hate them all."

She looked at me, her mouth working. She looked sullen and frightened and angry.

"They've been beastly to me always—always. From the very first. Why shouldn't I marry their precious father? What did it matter to *them*? They'd all got loads of money. *He* gave it to them. They wouldn't have had the brains to make any for themselves!"

She went on:

"Why shouldn't a man marry again—even if he is a bit old?

51

And he wasn't really old at all—not in himself. I was very fond of him. I *was* fond of him." She looked at me defiantly.

"I see," I said. "I see."

"I suppose you don't believe that—but it's true. I was sick of men. I wanted to have a home—I wanted someone to make a fuss of me and say nice things to me. Aristide said lovely things to me—and he could make you laugh—and he was clever. He thought up all sorts of smart ways to get round all these silly regulations. He was very, very clever. I'm not glad he's dead. I'm sorry."

She leaned back on the sofa. She had rather a wide mouth; it curled up sideways in a queer, sleepy smile.

"I've been happy here. I've been safe. I went to all those posh dressmakers—the ones I'd read about. I was as good as anybody. And Aristide gave me lovely things." She stretched out a hand, looking at the ruby on it.

Just for a moment I saw the hand and arm like an outstretched cat's claw, and heard her voice as a purr. She was still smiling to herself.

"What's wrong with that?" she demanded. "I was nice to him. I made him happy." She leaned forward. "Do you know how I met him?"

She went on without waiting for an answer.

"It was in the Gay Shamrock. He'd ordered scrambled eggs on toast and when I brought them to him I was crying. 'Sit down,' he said, 'and tell me what's the matter.' 'Oh, I couldn't,' I said. 'I'd get the sack if I did a thing like that.' 'No, you won't,' he said, 'I own this place.' I looked at him then. Such an odd little man he was, I thought at first—but he'd got a sort of power. I told him all about it. . . . You'll have heard about it all from *them*, I expect—making out I was a regular bad lot—but I wasn't. I was brought up very carefully. We had a shop—a very high-class shop—art needlework. I was never the sort of girl who had a lot of boy friends or made herself cheap. But Terry was different. He was Irish—and he was going overseas. . . He never wrote or anything—I suppose I was a fool. So there it was, you see. I was in trouble—just like some dreadful little servant girl. . . ."

Her voice was disdainful in its snobbery.

"Aristide was wonderful. He said everything would be all right. He said he was lonely. We'd be married at once, he said. It was like a dream. And then I found out he was the great Mr. Leonides. He owned masses of shops and restaurants and night clubs. It was quite like a fairy tale, wasn't it?"

"One kind of a fairy tale," I said dryly.

"We were married at a little church in the City—and then we went abroad."

She looked at me with eyes that came back from a long distance.

"There wasn't a child after all. It was all a mistake."

She smiled, the curled-up sideways, crooked smile.

"I vowed to myself that I'd be a really good wife to him, and I *was*. I ordered all the kinds of food he liked, and wore the colours he fancied and I did all I could to please him. And he was happy. But we never got rid of that family of his. Always coming and sponging and living in his pocket. Old Miss de Haviland—I think she ought to have gone away when he got married. I said so. But Aristide said, 'She's been here so long. It's her home now.' The truth is he liked to have them all about and underfoot. They were beastly to *me*, but he never seemed to notice that or to mind about it. Roger hates me—have you seen Roger? He's always hated me. He's jealous. And Philip's so stuck up he never speaks to me. And now they're trying to pretend I murdered him—and I didn't—I *didn't*!" She leaned towards me. "Please believe I didn't."

I found her very pathetic. The contemptuous way the Leonides family had spoken of her, their eagerness to believe that she had committed the crime—now, at this moment, it all seemed positively inhuman conduct. She was alone, defenceless, hunted down.

"And if it's not me, they think it's Laurence," she went on.

"What about Laurence?" I asked.

"I'm terribly sorry for Laurence. He's delicate and he couldn't go and fight. It's not because he was a coward. It's because he's sensitive. I've tried to cheer him up and to make him feel happy. He has to teach those horrible children. Eustace is always sneering at him, and Josephine—well, you've seen Josephine. You know what she's like."

I said I hadn't met Josephine yet.

"Sometimes I think that child isn't right in her head. She has horrible sneaky ways, and she looks queer. . . . She gives me the shivers sometimes."

I didn't want to talk about Josephine. I harked back to Laurence Brown.

"Who is he?" I asked. "Where does he come from?"

I had phrased it clumsily. She flushed.

"He isn't anybody particular. He's just like me. . . . What chance have we got against all of *them*?"

"Don't you think you're being a little hysterical?"

"No, I don't. They want to make out that Laurence did it —or that I did. They've got that policeman on their side. What chance have I got?"

"You mustn't work yourself up," I said.

"Why shouldn't it be one of them who killed him? Or someone from outside? Or one of the servants?"

"There's a certain lack of motive."

"Oh, *motive*! What motive had *I* got? Or Laurence?"

I felt rather uncomfortable as I said:

"They might think, I suppose, that you and—er—Laurence —are in love with each other—that you wanted to marry."

She sat bolt upright.

"That's a wicked thing to suggest! And it's not true! We've never said a word of that kind to each other. I've just been sorry for him and tried to cheer him up. We've been friends, that's all. You do believe me, don't you?"

I did believe her. That is, I believed that she and Laurence were, as she put it, only friends. But I also believed that, possibly unknown to herself, she was actually in love with the young man.

It was with that thought in my mind that I went downstairs in search of Sophia.

As I was about to go into the drawing-room, Sophia poked her head out of a door farther along the passage.

"Hallo," she said. "I'm helping Nannie with lunch."

I would have joined her, but she came out into the passage, shut the door behind her, and taking my arm led me into the drawing-room, which was empty.

"Well," she said, "did you see Brenda? What did you think of her?"

"Frankly," I said, "I was sorry for her."

Sophia looked amused.

"I see," she said. "So she got you."

I felt slightly irritated.

"The point is," I said, "that I can see her side of it. Apparently you can't."

"Her side of what?"

"Honestly, Sophia, have any of the family ever been nice to her, or even fairly decent to her, since she came here?"

"No, we haven't been nice to her. Why should we be?"

"Just ordinary Christian kindliness, if nothing else."

"What a very high moral tone you're taking, Charles. Brenda must have done her stuff pretty well."

"Really, Sophia, you seem—I don't know what's come over you."

"I'm just being honest and not pretending. You've seen Brenda's side of it, so you say. Now take a look at my side. I don't like the type of young woman who makes up a hard-luck story and marries a very rich old man on the strength of it. I've a perfect right not to like that type of young woman, and there is no earthly reason why I should pretend I do. And if the facts were written down in cold blood on paper, *you* wouldn't like that young woman either."

"Was it a made-up story?" I asked.

"About the child? I don't know. Personally, I think so."

"And you resent the fact that your grandfather was taken in by it?"

"Oh, grandfather wasn't taken in." Sophia laughed. "Grandfather was never taken in by anybody. He wanted Brenda. He wanted to play Cophetua to her beggar-maid. He knew just what he was doing and it worked out beautifully according to plan. From grandfather's point of view the marriage was a complete success—like all his other operations."

"Was engaging Laurence Brown as tutor another of your grandfather's successes?" I asked ironically.

Sophia frowned.

"Do you know, I'm not sure that it wasn't. He wanted to keep Brenda happy and amused. He may have thought that jewels and clothes weren't enough. He may have thought she wanted a mild romance in her life. He may have calculated that someone like Laurence Brown, somebody really *tame*, if you know what I mean, would just do the trick. A beautiful soulful friendship tinged with melancholy that would stop Brenda from having a real affair with someone outside. I wouldn't put it past grandfather to have worked out something on those lines. He was rather an old devil, you know."

55

"He must have been," I said.

"He couldn't, of course, have visualised that it would lead to murder. . . . And that," said Sophia, speaking with sudden vehemence, "is really why I don't, much as I would like to, really believe that she did it. If she'd planned to murder him—or if she and Laurence had planned it together —grandfather would have known about it. I dare say that seems a bit far-fetched to you——"

"I must confess it does," I said.

"But then you didn't know grandfather. He certainly wouldn't have connived at his own murder! So there you are! Up against a blank wall."

"She's frightened, Sophia," I said. "She's very frightened."

"Chief-Inspector Taverner and his merry, merry men? Yes, I dare say they are rather alarming. Laurence, I suppose, is in hysterics?"

"Practically. He made, I thought, a disgusting exhibition of himself. I don't understand what a woman can see in a man like that."

"Don't you, Charles? Actually Laurence has a lot of sex appeal."

"A weakling like that," I said incredulously.

"Why do men always think that a caveman must necessarily be the only type of person attractive to the opposite sex? Laurence has got sex appeal all right— but I wouldn't expect you to be aware of it." She looked at me. "Brenda got her hooks into you all right."

"Don't be absurd. She's not even really good-looking. And she certainly didn't——"

"Display allure? No, she just made you sorry for her. She's not actually beautiful, she's not in the least clever— but she's got one very outstanding characteristic. She can make trouble. She's made trouble, already, between you and me."

"Sophia!" I cried aghast.

Sophia went to the door.

"Forget it, Charles. I must get on with lunch."

"I'll come and help."

"No, you stay here. It will rattle Nannie to have 'a gentleman in the kitchen'."

"Sophia," I called as she went out.

"Yes, what is it?"

"Just a servant problem. Why haven't you got any servants

56

down here and upstairs something in an apron and a cap opened the door to us?"

"Grandfather had a cook, housemaid, parlourmaid, and valet-attendant. He liked servants. He paid them the earth, of course, and he got them. Clemency and Roger just have a daily woman who comes in and cleans. They don't like servants—or rather Clemency doesn't. If Roger didn't get a square meal in the City every day, he'd starve. Clemency's idea of a meal is lettuce, tomatoes, and raw carrot. We sometimes have servants, and then mother throws one of her temperaments and they leave, and we have dailies for a bit and then start again. We're in the daily period. Nannie is the permanency and copes in emergencies. Now you know."

Sophia went out. I sank down in one of the large brocaded chairs and gave myself up to speculation.

Upstairs I had seen Brenda's side of it. Here and now I had been shown Sophia's side of it. I realised completely the justice of Sophia's point of view—what might be called the Leonides family's point of view. They resented a stranger within the gates who had obtained admission by what they regarded as ignoble means. They were entirely within their rights. As Sophia had said: on paper it wouldn't look well . . .

But there was the human side of it—the side that I saw and that they didn't. They were, they always had been, rich and well established. They had no conception of the temptations of the underdog. Brenda Leonides had wanted wealth, and pretty things and safety—and a home. She had claimed that in exchange she had made her old husband happy. I had sympathy with her. Certainly, while I was talking with her, I had had sympathy for her. . . . Had I got as much sympathy now?

Two sides to the question—different angles of vision—which was the true angle . . . the true angle. . . .

I had slept very little the night before. I had been up early to accompany Taverner. Now, in the warm, flower-scented atmosphere of Magda Leonides' drawing-room, my body relaxed in the cushioned embrace of the big chair and my eyelids dropped . . .

Thinking of Brenda, of Sophia, of an old man's picture, my thoughts slid together into a pleasant haze.

I slept. . . .

X

I RETURNED to consciousness so gradually that I didn't at first realise that I had been asleep.

The scent of flowers was in my nose. In front of me a round white blob appeared to float in space. It was some few seconds before I realised that it was a human face I was looking at—a face suspended in the air about a foot or two away from me. As my faculties returned, my vision became more precise. The face still had its goblin suggestion—it was round with a bulging brow, combed-back hair and small, rather beady, black eyes. But it was definitely attached to a body—a small skinny body. It was regarding me very earnestly.

"Hallo," it said.

"Hallo," I replied, blinking.

"I'm Josephine."

I had already deduced that. Sophia's sister, Josephine, was, I judged, about eleven or twelve years of age. She was a fantastically ugly child with a very distinct likeness to her grandfather. It seemed to me possible that she also had his brains.

"You're Sophia's young man," said Josephine.

I acknowledged the correctness of this remark.

"But you came down here with Chief-Inspector Taverner. Why did you come with Chief-Inspector Taverner?"

"He's a friend of mine."

"Is he? I don't like him. I shan't tell him things."

"What sort of things?"

"The things I know. I know a lot of things. I like knowing things."

She sat down on the arm of the chair and continued her searching scrutiny of my face. I began to feel quite uncomfortable.

"Grandfather's been murdered. Did you know?"

"Yes," I said. "I knew."

"He was poisoned. With es-er-ine." She pronounced the word very carefully. "It's interesting, isn't it?"

"I suppose it is.'

"Eustace and I are very interested. We like detective stories. I've always wanted to be a detective. I'm being one now. I'm collecting clues."

She was, I felt, rather a ghoulish child.

She returned to the charge.

"The man who came with Chief-Inspector Taverner is a
detective too, isn't he? In books it says you can always know
plain-clothes detectives by their boots. But this detective was
wearing suède shoes."

"The old order changeth," I said.

Josephine interpreted this remark according to her own ideas.

"Yes," she said, "there will be a lot of changes here now, I
expect. We shall go and live in a house in London on the
Embankment. Mother has wanted to for a long time. She'll be
very pleased. I don't expect father will mind if his books
go, too. He couldn't afford it before. He lost an awful lot of
money over *Jezebel*."

"*Jezebel*?" I queried.

"Yes, didn't you see it?"

"Oh, it was a play? No, I didn't. I've been abroad."

"It didn't run very long. Actually it was the most awful
flop. I don't think mother's really the type to play Jezebel, do
you?"

I balanced my impressions of Magda. Neither in the peach-
coloured *négligé* nor in the tailored suit had she conveyed any
suggestion of Jezebel, but I was willing to believe that there
were other Magdas that I had not yet seen.

"Perhaps not," I said cautiously.

"Grandfather always said it would be a flop. He said
he wouldn't put up any money for one of those historical
religious plays. He said it would never be a box-office success.
But mother was frightfully keen. I didn't like it much myself.
It wasn't really a bit like the story in the Bible. I mean,
Jezebel wasn't wicked like she is in the Bible. She was
all patriotic and really quite nice. That made it dull. Still, the
end was all right. They threw her out of the window. Only
no dogs came and ate her. I think that was a pity, don't
you? I like the part about the dogs eating her best.
Mother says you can't have dogs on the stage but I don't
see why. You could have performing dogs." She quoted with
gusto: "'*And they ate her all but the palms of her hands.*'
Why didn't they eat the palms of her hands?"

"I've really no idea," I said.

"You wouldn't think, would you, that dogs were so
particular. Our dogs aren't. They eat simply *anything*."

Josephine brooded on this Biblical mystery for some seconds.

"I'm sorry the play was a flop," I said.

"Yes. Mother was terribly upset. The notices were simply frightful. When she read them, she burst into tears and cried all day and she threw her breakfast tray at Gladys, and Gladys gave notice. It was rather fun."

"I perceive that you like drama, Josephine," I said.

"They did a post-mortem on grandfather," said Josephine. "To find out what he had died of. A P.M., they call it, but I think that's rather confusing, don't you? Because P.M. stands for Prime Minister too. And for afternoon," she added thoughtfully.

"Are you sorry your grandfather is dead?" I asked.

"Not particularly. I didn't like him much. He stopped me learning to be a ballet dancer."

"Did you want to learn ballet dancing?"

"Yes, and mother was willing for me to learn, and father didn't mind, but grandfather said I'd be no good."

She slipped off the arm of the chair, kicked off her shoes and endeavoured to get on to what are called technically, I believe, her points.

"You have to have the proper shoes, of course," she explained, "and even then you get frightful abscesses sometimes on the ends of your toes." She resumed her shoes and inquired casually:

"Do you like this house?"

"I'm not quite sure," I said.

"I suppose it will be sold now. Unless Brenda goes on living in it. And I suppose Uncle Roger and Aunt Clemency won't be going away now."

"Were they going away?" I asked with a faint stirring of interest.

"Yes. They were going on Tuesday. Abroad, somewhere. They were going by air. Aunt Clemency bought one of those new featherweight cases."

"I hadn't heard they were going abroad," I said.

"No," said Josephine. "Nobody knew. It was a secret. They weren't going to tell anyone until after they'd gone. They were going to leave a note behind for grandfather."

She added:

"Not pinned to the pin-cushion. That's only in very old

60

shioned books and wives do it when they leave their
usbands. But it would be silly now because nobody has
n-cushions any more."

"Of course they don't. Josephine, do you know why your
ncle Roger was—going away?"

She shot me a cunning sideways glance.

"I think I do. It was something to do with Uncle Roger's
ffice in London. I rather think—but I'm not sure—that
e'd *embezzled* something."

"What makes you think that?"

Josephine came nearer and breathed heavily in my face.

"The day that grandfather was poisoned Uncle Roger was
ut up in his room with him ever so long. They were talking
nd talking. And Uncle Roger was saying that he'd never
een any good, and that he'd let grandfather down—and that
 wasn't the money so much—it was the feeling he'd been
nworthy of trust. He was in an awful state."

I looked at Josephine with mixed feelings.

"Josephine," I said, "hasn't anybody ever told you that
's not nice to listen at doors?"

Josephine nodded her head vigorously.

"Of course they have. But if you want to find things out,
ou *have* to listen at doors. I bet Chief-Inspector Taverner
oes, don't you?"

I considered the point. Josephine went on vehemently:

"And anyway, if *he* doesn't, the other one does, the
ne with the suède shoes. And they look in people's desks
nd read all their letters, and find out all their secrets. Only
hey're stupid! They don't know where to look!"

Josephine spoke with cold superiority. I was stupid enough
o let the inference escape me. The unpleasant child went on:

"Eustace and I know lots of things—but I know more
han Eustace does. And I shan't tell him. He says women
an't ever be great detectives. But I say they can. I'm going to
rite down everything in a notebook and then, when the
olice are completely baffled, I shall come forward and say,
I can tell you who did it.'"

"Do you read a lot of detective stories, Josephine?"

"Masses."

"I suppose you think you know who killed your grand-
ather?"

"Well, I *think* so—but I shall have to find a few more

61

clues." She paused and added: "Chief-Inspector Tavern
thinks that Brenda did it, doesn't he? Or Brenda an
Laurence together because they're in love with each other."

"You shouldn't say things like that, Josephine."

"Why not? They are in love with each other."

"You can't possibly judge."

"Yes, I can. They write to each other. Love letters."

"Josephine! How do you know that?"

"Because I've read them. Awfully soppy letters. But Lau
ence is soppy. He was too frightened to fight in the war. H
went into basements, and stoked boilers. When the flyin,
bombs went over here, he used to turn green—really green.
made Eustace and me laugh a lot."

What I would have said next I do not know, for at th;
moment a car drew up outside. In a flash Josephine was ;
the window, her snub nose pressed to the pane.

"Who is it?" I asked.

"It's Mr. Gaitskill, grandfather's lawyer. I expect he
come about the will."

Breathing excitedly, she hurried from the room, doubtle
to resume her sleuthing activities.

Magda Leonides came into the room, and to my surpri;
came across to me and took my hands in hers.

"My dear," she said, "thank goodness you're still her
One *needs* a man so badly."

She dropped my hands, crossed to a high-backed chai
altered its position a little, glanced at herself in a mirro
then, picking up a small Battersea enamel box from
table, she stood pensively opening and shutting it.

It was an attractive pose.

Sophia put her head in at the door and said in a
admonitory whisper, "Gaitskill!"

"I know," said Magda.

A few moments later Sophia entered the room, accom
panied by a small elderly man, and Magda put down he
enamel box and came forward to meet him.

"Good morning, Mrs. Philip. I'm on my way upstairs.
seems there's some misunderstanding about the will. You
husband wrote to me with the impression that the will wa
in my keeping. I understood from Mr. Leonides himself th;
it was at his vault. You don't know anything about it,
suppose?"

"About poor Sweetie's will?" Magda opened astonished eyes. "No, of course not. Don't tell me that wicked woman upstairs has destroyed it?"

"Now, Mrs. Philip,"—he shook an admonitory finger at her—"no wild surmises. It's just a question of where your father-in-law kept it."

"But he sent it to you—surely he did—after signing it. He actually told us he had."

"The police, I understand, have been through Mr. Leonides' private papers," said Mr. Gaitskill. "I'll just have a word with Chief-Inspector Taverner."

He left the room.

"Darling," cried Magda. "She *has* destroyed it. I know I'm right."

"Nonsense, Mother, she wouldn't do a stupid thing like that."

"It wouldn't be stupid at all. If there's no will she'll get everything."

"Ssh—here's Gaitskill back again."

The lawyer re-entered the room. Chief-Inspector Taverner was with him and behind Taverner came Philip.

"I understood from Mr. Leonides," Gaitskill was saying, "that he had placed his will with the Bank for safe keeping."

Taverner shook his head.

"I've been in communication with the Bank. They have no private papers belonging to Mr. Leonides beyond certain securities which they held for him."

Philip said:

"I wonder if Roger—or Aunt Edith. . . . Perhaps, Sophia, you'd ask them to come down here."

But Roger Leonides, summoned with the others to the conclave, could give no assistance.

"But it's nonsense—absolute nonsense," he declared. "Father signed the will and said distinctly that he was posting it to Mr. Gaitskill on the following day."

"If my memory serves me," said Mr. Gaitskill, leaning back and half-closing his eyes, "it was on November 24th of last year that I forwarded a draft drawn up according to Mr. Leonides' instructions. He approved the draft, returned it to me, and in due course I sent him the will for signature. After a lapse of a week, I ventured to remind him that I had not yet received the will duly signed and attested, and asking

63

him if there was anything he wished altered. He replied that he was perfectly satisfied, and added that after signing the will he had sent it to his bank."

"That's quite right," said Roger eagerly. "It was about the end of November last year—you remember, Philip? Father had us all up one evening and read the will to us."

Taverner turned towards Philip Leonides.

"That agrees with your recollection, Mr. Leonides?"

"Yes," said Philip.

"It was rather like the Voysey Inheritance," said Magda. She sighed pleasurably. "I always think there's something so dramatic about a will."

"Miss Sophia?"

"Yes," said Sophia. "I remember perfectly."

"And the provisions of that will?" asked Taverner.

Mr. Gaitskill was about to reply in his precise fashion, but Roger Leonides got ahead of him.

"It was a perfectly simple will. Electra and Joyce had died and their share of the settlements had returned to father. Joyce's son, William, had been killed in action in Burma, and the money he left went to his father. Philip and I and the children were the only relatives left. Father explained that. He left fifty thousand pounds free of duty to Aunt Edith, a hundred thousand pounds free of duty to Brenda, this house to Brenda, or else a suitable house in London to be purchased for her, whichever she preferred. The residue to be divided into three portions, one to myself, one to Philip, the third to be divided between Sophia, Eustace, and Josephine, the portions of the last two to be held in trust until they should come of age. I think that's right, isn't it, Mr. Gaitskill?"

"Those are—roughly stated—the provisions of the document I drew up," agreed Mr. Gaitskill, displaying some slight acerbity at not having been allowed to speak for himself.

"Father read it out to us," said Roger. "He asked if there was any comment we might like to make. Of course there was none."

"Brenda made a comment," said Miss de Haviland.

"Yes," said Magda with zest. "She said she couldn't bear her darling old Aristide to talk about death. It 'gave her the creeps,' she said. And after he was dead she didn't want any of the horrid money!"

"That," said Miss de Haviland, "was a conventional protest, typical of her class."

It was a cruel and biting little remark. I realised suddenly how much Edith de Haviland disliked Brenda.

"A very fair and reasonable disposal of his estate," said Mr. Gaitskill.

"And after reading it what happened?" asked Inspector Taverner.

"After reading it," said Roger, "he signed it."

Taverner leaned forward.

"Just how and when did he sign it?"

Roger looked round at his wife in an appealing way. Clemency spoke in answer to that look. The rest of the family seemed content for her to do so.

"You want to know exactly what took place?"

"If you please, Mrs. Roger."

"My father-in-law laid the will down on his desk and requested one of us—Roger, I think—to ring the bell. Roger did so. When Johnson came in answer to the bell, my father-in-law requested him to fetch Janet Wolmer, the parlourmaid. When they were both there, he signed the will and requested them to sign their own names beneath his signature."

"The correct procedure," said Mr. Gaitskill. "A will must be signed by the testator in the presence of two witnesses who must affix their own signatures at the same time and place."

"And after that?" asked Taverner.

"My father-in-law thanked them, and they went out. My father-in-law picked up the will, put it in a long envelope and mentioned that he would send it to Mr. Gaitskill on the following day."

"You all agree," said Inspector Taverner, looking round, "that this is an accurate account of what happened?"

There were murmurs of agreement.

"The will was on the desk, you said. How near were any of you to that desk?"

"Not very near. Five or six yards, perhaps, would be the nearest."

"When Mr. Leonides read you the will was he himself sitting at the desk?"

"Yes."

"Did he get up, or leave the desk, after reading the will and before signing it?"

"No."

"Could the servants read the document when they signed their names?"

"No," said Clemency. "My father-in-law placed a sheet of paper across the upper part of the document."

"Quite properly," said Philip. "The contents of the will were no business of the servants."

"I see," said Taverner. "At least—I don't see."

With a brisk movement he produced a long envelope and leaned forward to hand it to the lawyer.

"Have a look at that," he said. "And tell me what it is."

Mr. Gaitskill drew a folded document out of the envelope. He looked at it with lively astonishment, turning it round and round in his hands.

"This," he said, "is somewhat surprising. I do not understand it at all. Where was this, if I may ask?"

"In the safe, amongst Mr. Leonides' other papers."

"But what is it?" demanded Roger. "What's all the fuss about?"

"This is the will I prepared for your father's signature, Roger—but—I can't understand it after what you have all said —it is not signed. '

"What? Well, I suppose it is just a draft."

"No," said the lawyer. "Mr. Leonides returned me the original draft. I then drew up the will—*this* will," he tapped it with his finger—"and sent it to him for signature. According to your evidence he signed the will in front of you all—and two witnesses also appended their signatures—and yet this will is unsigned."

"But that's impossible," exclaimed Philip Leonides, speaking with more animation that I had yet heard from him.

Taverner asked: "How good was your father's eyesight?"

"He suffered from glaucoma. He used strong glasses, of course, for reading."

"He had those glasses on that evening?"

"Certainly. He didn't take his glasses off until after he had signed. I think I am right?"

"Quite right," said Clemency.

"And nobody—you are all sure of that—went near the desk before the signing of the will?"

"I wonder now," said Magda, screwing up her eyes. "If one could only visualise it all again."

"Nobody went near the desk," said Sophia. "And grandfather sat at it all the time."

"The desk was in the position it is now? It was not near a door, or a window, or any drapery?"

"It was where it is now."

"I am trying to see how a substitution of some kind could be effected," said Taverner. "Some kind of substitution there must have been. Mr. Leonides was under the impression that he was signing the document he had just read aloud."

"Couldn't the signatures have been erased?" Roger demanded.

"No, Mr. Leonides. Not without leaving signs of erasion. There is one other possibility. That this is not the document sent to Mr. Leonides by Mr. Gaitskill and which he signed in your presence."

"On the contrary," said Mr. Gaitskill. "I could swear to this being the original document. There is a small flaw in the paper—at the top left-hand corner—it resembles, by a stretch of fancy, an aeroplane. I noticed it at the time."

The family looked blankly at one another.

"A most curious set of circumstances," said Mr. Gaitskill. "Quite without precedent in my experience."

"The whole thing's impossible," said Roger. "We were all there. It simply couldn't have happened."

Miss de Haviland gave a dry cough.

"Never any good wasting breath saying something that has happened couldn't have happened," she remarked. "What's the position now? That's what I'd like to know."

Gaitskill immediately became the cautious lawyer.

"The position will have to be examined very carefully," he said. "This document, of course, revokes all former wills and testaments. There are a large number of witnesses who saw Mr. Leonides sign what he certainly believed to be this will in perfectly good faith. Hum. Very interesting. Quite a little legal problem."

Taverner glanced at his watch.

"I'm afraid," he said, "I've been keeping you from your lunch."

"Won't you stay and lunch with us, Chief-Inspector?" asked Philip.

"Thank you, Mr. Leonides, but I am meeting Dr. Gray in Swinley Dean."

Philip turned to the lawyer.

"You'll lunch with us, Gaitskill?"

"Thank you, Philip."

Everybody stood up. I edged unobtrusively towards Sophia.

"Do I go or stay?" I murmured. It sounded ridiculously like the title of a Victorian song.

"Go, I think," said Sophia.

I slipped quietly out of the room in pursuit of Taverner. Josephine was swinging to and fro on a baize door leading to the back quarters. She appeared to be highly amused about something.

"The police are stupid," she observed.

Sophia came out of the drawing-room.

"What have you been doing, Josephine?"

"Helping Nannie."

"I believe you've been listening outside the door."

Josephine made a face at her and retreated.

"That child," said Sophia, "is a bit of a problem."

XI

I CAME into the A.C.'s room at the Yard to find Taverner finishing the recital of what had apparently been a tale of woe.

"And there you are," he was saying. "I've turned the lot of them inside out—and what do I get—nothing at all! No motives. None of them hard up. And all that we've got against the wife and her young man is that he made sheep's eyes at her when she poured him out his coffee!"

"Come, come, Taverner," I said. "I can do a little better than that for you."

"You can, can you? Well, Mr. Charles, what did *you* get?"

I sat down, lit a cigarette, leaned back and let them have it.

"Roger Leonides and his wife were planning a getaway abroad next Tuesday. Roger and his father had a stormy interview on the day of the old man's death. Old Leonides had found out something was wrong, and Roger was admitting culpability."

Taverner went purple in the face.

"Where the hell did you get all that from?" he demanded. "If you got it from the servants——"

"I didn't get it from the servants. I got it," I said, "from a private inquiry agent."

"What do you mean?"

"And I must say that, in accordance with the canons of the best detective stories, he, or rather she—or perhaps I'd better say it—has licked the police hollow!

"I also think," I went on, "that my private detective has a few more things up his, her or its sleeve."

Taverner opened his mouth and shut it again. He wanted to ask so many questions at once that he found it hard to begin.

"Roger!" he said. "So Roger's a wrong 'un, is he?"

I felt a slight reluctance as I unburdened myself. I had liked Roger Leonides. Remembering his comfortable, friendly room, and the man's own friendly charm, I disliked setting the hounds of justice on his track. It was possible, of course, that all Josephine's information would be unreliable, but I did not really think so.

"So the kid told you?" said Taverner. "She seems to be wise to everything that goes on in that house."

"Children usually are," said my father dryly.

This information, if true, altered the whole position. If Roger had been, as Josephine had confidently suggested, "embezzling" the funds of Associated Catering and if the old man had found it out, it might have been vital to silence old Leonides and to leave England before the truth came out. Possibly Roger had rendered himself liable to criminal prosecution.

It was agreed that inquiries should be made without delay into the affairs of Associated Catering.

"It will be an almighty crash, if that goes," my father remarked. "It's a huge concern. There are millions involved."

"If it's really in Queer Street, it gives us what we want," said Taverner. "Father summons Roger. Roger breaks down and confesses. Brenda Leonides was out at a cinema. Roger has only got to leave his father's room, walk into the bathroom, empty out an insulin phial and replace it with the strong solution of eserine and there you are. Or his wife may have done it. She went over to the other wing after she came home that day—says she went to fetch a pipe Roger had left there. But she could have gone over to switch the

69

stuff before Brenda came home and gave him his injection. She'd be quite cool and capable about it."

I nodded. "Yes, I fancy her as the actual doer of the deed. She's cool enough for anything! And I don't really think that Roger Leonides would think of poison as a means—that trick with the insulin has something feminine about it."

"Plenty of men poisoners," said my father dryly.

"Oh, I know, sir," said Taverner. "Don't I know!" he added with feeling.

"All the same I shouldn't have said Roger was the type."

"Pritchard," the Old Man reminded him, "was a good mixer."

"Let's say they were in it together."

"With the accent on Lady Macbeth," said my father, as Taverner departed. "Is that how she strikes you, Charles?"

I visualised the slight, graceful figure standing by the window in that austere room.

"Not quite," I said. "Lady Macbeth was essentially a greedy woman. I don't think Clemency Leonides is. I don't think she wants or cares for possessions."

"But she might care, desperately, about her husband's safety?"

"That, yes. And she could certainly be—well, ruthless."

"*Different kinds of ruthlessness . . .*" That was what Sophia had said.

I looked up to see the Old Man watching me.

"What's in your mind, Charles?"

But I didn't tell him then.

I was summoned on the following day and found Taverner and my father together.

Taverner was looking pleased with himself and slightly excited.

"Associated Catering is on the rocks," said my father.

"Due to crash at any minute," said Taverner.

"I saw there had been a sharp fall in the shares last night," I said. "But they seem to have recovered this morning."

"We've had to go about it very cautiously," said Taverner. "No direct inquiries. Nothing to cause a panic—or to put the wind up our absconding gentleman. But we've got certain private sources of information and the information is fairly definite. Associated Catering is on the verge of a crash. It can't possibly meet its commitments. The truth seems to be that it's been grossly mismanaged for years."

"By Roger Leonides?"

"Yes. He's had supreme power, you know."

"And he's helped himself to money——"

"No," said Taverner. "We don't think he has. To put it bluntly, he may be a murderer, but we don't think he's a swindler. Quite frankly he's just been—a fool. He doesn't seem to have had any kind of judgment. He's launched out where he ought to have held in—he's hesitated and retreated where he ought to have launched out. He's delegated power to the last sort of people he ought to have delegated it to. He's a trustful sort of chap, and he's trusted the wrong people. At every time, and on every occasion, he's done the wrong thing."

"There are people like that," said my father. "And they're not really stupid either. They're bad judges of men, that's all. And they're enthusiastic at the wrong time."

"A man like that oughtn't to be in business at all," said Taverner.

"He probably wouldn't be," said my father, "except for the accident of being Aristide Leonides' son."

"That show was absolutely blooming when the old man handed it over to him. It ought to have been a gold mine! You'd think he could have just sat back and let the show run itself."

"No;" my father shook his head. "No show runs itself. There are always decisions to be made—a man sacked here —a man appointed there—small questions of policy. And with Roger Leonides the answer seems to have been always wrong."

"That's right," said Taverner. "He's a loyal sort of chap, for one thing. He kept on the most frightful duds—just because he had an affection for them—or because they'd been there a long time. And then he sometimes had wild impractical ideas and insisted on trying them out in spite of the enormous outlay involved."

"But nothing criminal?" my father insisted.

"No, nothing criminal."

"Then why murder?" I asked.

"He may have been a fool and not a knave," said Taverner. "But the result was the same—or nearly the same. The only thing that could save Associated Catering from the smash was a really colossal sum of money by next" (he consulted a notebook) "by next Wednesday at the latest."

"Such a sum as he would inherit, or thought he would have inherited, under his father's will?"

"Exactly."

"But he wouldn't be able to have got that sum in cash."

"No. But he'd have got credit. It's the same thing."

The Old Man nodded.

"Wouldn't it have been simpler to go to old Leonides and ask for help?" he suggested.

"I think he did," said Taverner. "I think that's what the kid overheard. The old boy refused point blank, I should imagine, to throw good money after bad. He would, you know."

I thought that Taverner was right there. Aristide Leonides had refused the backing for Magda's play—he had said that it would not be a box-office success. Events had proved him correct. He was a generous man to his family, but he was not a man to waste money in unprofitable enterprises. And Associated Catering ran to thousands, or probably hundreds of thousands. He had refused point blank, and the only way for Roger to avoid financial ruin was for his father to die.

Yes, there was certainly a motive there all right.

My father looked at his watch.

"I've asked him to come here," he said. "He'll be here any minute now."

"Roger?"

"Yes.'

"Will you walk into my parlour, said the spider to the fly?" I murmured.

Taverner looked at me in a shocked way.

"We shall give him all the proper cautions," he said severely.

The stage was set, the shorthand writer established. Presently the buzzer sounded, and a few minutes later Roger Leonides entered the room.

He came in eagerly—and rather clumsily—he stumbled over a chair. I was reminded as before of a large friendly dog. At the same time I decided quite definitely that it was not he who had carried out the actual process of transferring eserine to an insulin bottle. He would have broken it, spilled

72

it, or muffed the operation in some way or the other. No, Clemency's, I decided, had been the actual hand, though Roger had been privy to the deed.

Words rushed from him.

"You wanted to see me? You've found out something? Hallo, Charles. I didn't see you. Nice of you to come along. But please tell me, Sir Arthur——"

Such a nice fellow—really such a nice fellow. But lots of murderers had been nice fellows—so their astonished friends had said afterwards. Feeling rather like Judas, I smiled a greeting.

My father was deliberate, coldly official. The glib phrases were uttered. Statement . . . taken down . . . no compulsion . . . solicitor . . .

Roger Leonides brushed them all aside with the same characteristic eager impatience.

I saw the faint sardonic smile on Chief-Inspector Taverner's face, and read from it the thought in his mind.

"*Always sure of themselves, these chaps.* They can't make a mistake. They're far too clever!"

I sat down unobtrusively in a corner and listened.

"I have asked you to come here, Mr. Leonides," my father said, "not to give you fresh information, but to ask for some information from you—information that you have previously withheld."

Roger Leonides looked bewildered.

"Withheld? But I've told you everything—absolutely everything!"

"I think not. You had a conversation with the deceased on the afternoon of his death?"

"Yes, yes, I had tea with him. I told you so."

"You told us that, yes, but you did not tell us about your conversation."

"We—just—talked."

"What about?"

"Daily happenings, the house, Sophia——"

"What about Associated Catering? Was that mentioned?"

I think I had hoped up to then that Josephine had been inventing the whole story; but if so, that hope was quickly quenched.

Roger's face changed. It changed in a moment from eagerness to something that was recognisably close to despair.

"Oh, my God," he said. He dropped into a chair and buried his face in his hands.

Taverner smiled like a contented cat.

"You admit, Mr. Leonides, that you have not been frank with us?"

"How did you get to know about that? I thought nobody knew—I don't see how anybody *could* know."

"We have means of finding out these things, Mr. Leonides." There was a majestic pause. "I think you will see now that you had better tell us the truth."

"Yes, yes, of course. I'll tell you. What do you want to know?"

"Is it true that Associated Catering is on the verge of collapse?"

"Yes. It can't be staved off now. The crash is bound to come. If only my father could have died without ever knowing. I feel so ashamed—so disgraced——"

"There is a possibility of criminal prosecution?"

Roger sat up sharply.

"No, indeed. It will be bankruptcy—but an honourable bankruptcy. Creditors will be paid twenty shillings in the pound if I throw in my personal assets, which I shall do. No, the disgrace I feel is to have failed my father. He trusted me. He made over to me this, his largest concern—and his pet concern. He never interfered, he never asked what I was doing. He just—trusted me . . . And I let him down."

My father said dryly:

"You say there was no likelihood of criminal prosecution? Why then had you and your wife planned to go abroad without telling anybody of your intention?"

"You know that too?"

"Yes, Mr. Leonides."

"But don't you see?" He leaned forward eagerly. "I couldn't face him with the truth. It would have looked, you see, as if I was asking for money. As though I wanted him to set me on my feet again. He—he was very fond of me. He would have wanted to help. But I couldn't—I couldn't go on—it would have meant making a mess of things all over again —I'm no good. I haven't got the ability. I'm not the man my father was. I've always known it. I've tried. But it's no good. I've been so miserable—God! you don't know how miserable I've been! Trying to get out of the muddle, hoping

74

I'd just get square, hoping the dear old man would never need to hear about it. And then it came—no more hope of avoiding the crash. Clemency—my wife—she understood, she agreed with me. We thought out this plan. Say nothing to anyone. Go away. And then let the storm break. I'd leave a letter for my father, telling him all about it—telling him how ashamed I was and begging him to forgive me. He's been so good to me always—you don't know! But it would be too late then for him to do anything. That's what I wanted. Not to ask him—or even to seem to ask him for help. Start again on my own somewhere. Live simply and humbly. Grow things. Coffee—fruit. Just have the bare necessities of life —hard on Clemency, but she swore she didn't mind. She's wonderful—absolutely wonderful."

"I see." My father's voice was dry. "And what made you change your mind?"

"Change my mind?"

"Yes. What made you decide to go to your father and ask for financial help after all?"

Roger stared at him.

"But I didn't!"

"Come now, Mr. Leonides."

"You've got it all wrong. I didn't go to him. *He* sent for *me*. He'd heard, somehow, in the City. A rumour, I suppose. But he always knew things. Someone had told him. He tackled me with it. Then, of course, I broke down . . . I told him everything. I said it wasn't so much the money—it was the feeling I'd let him down after he'd trusted me."

Roger swallowed convulsively.

"The dear old man," he said. "You can't imagine how good he was to me. No reproaches. Just kindness. I told him I didn't want help, that I preferred not to have it—that I'd rather go away as I'd planned to do. But he wouldn't listen. He insisted on coming to the rescue—on putting Associated Catering on its legs again."

Taverner said sharply:

"You are asking us to believe that your father intended to come to your assistance financially?"

"Certainly he did. He wrote to his brokers then and there, giving them instructions."

I suppose he saw the incredulity on the two men's faces. He flushed.

"Look here," he said, "I've still got the letter. I was to post it. But of course later—with—with the shock and confusion, I forgot. I've probably got it in my pocket now."

He drew out his wallet and started hunting through it. Finally he found what he wanted. It was a creased envelope with a stamp on it. It was addressed, as I saw by leaning forward, to Messrs. Greatorex and Hanbury.

"Read it for yourselves," he said, "if you don't believe me."

My father tore open the letter. Taverner went round behind him. I did not see the letter then, but I saw it later. It instructed Messrs. Greatorex and Hanbury to realise certain investments and asked for a member of the firm to be sent down on the following day to take certain instructions *re* the affairs of Associated Catering. Some of it was unintelligible to me, but its purpose was clear enough. Aristide Leonides was preparing to put Associated Catering on its feet again.

Taverner said:

"We will give you a receipt for this, Mr. Leonides."

Roger took the receipt. He got up and said:

"Is that all? You do see how it all was, don't you?"

Taverner said:

"Mr. Leonides gave you this letter and then you left him? What did you do next?"

"I rushed back to my own part of the house. My wife had just come in. I told her what my father proposed to do. How wonderful he had been! I—really, I hardly knew what I was doing."

"And your father was taken ill—how long after that?"

"Let me see—half an hour, perhaps, or an hour. Brenda came rushing in. She was frightened. She said he looked queer. I—I rushed over with her. But I've told you all this before."

"During your former visit, did you go into the bathroom adjoining your father's room at all?"

"I don't think so. No—no, I am sure I didn't. Why, you can't possibly think that I——"

My father quelled the sudden indignation. He got up and shook hands.

"Thank you, Mr. Leonides," he said. "You have been very helpful. But you should have told us all this before."

The door closed behind Roger. I got up and came to look at the letter lying on my father's table.

"It *could* be a forgery," said Taverner hopefully.

"It could be," said my father, "but I don't think it is. I think we'll have to accept it exactly as it stands. Old Leonides was prepared to get his son out of this mess. It could have been done more efficiently by him alive than it could by Roger after his death—especially as it now transpires that no will is to be found and that in consequence Roger's actual amount of inheritance is open to question. That means delays—and difficulties. As things now stand, the crash is bound to come. No, Taverner, Roger Leonides and his wife had no motive for getting the old man out of the way. On the contrary——"

He stopped and repeated thoughtfully as though a sudden thought had occurred to him: "On the contrary , . ."

"What's on your mind, sir?" Taverner asked.

The Old Man said slowly:

"If Aristide Leonides had lived only another twenty-four hours, Roger would have been all right. But he didn't live twenty-four hours. He died suddenly and dramatically within little more than an hour."

"H'm," said Taverner. "Do you think somebody in the house *wanted* Roger to go broke? Someone who had an opposing financial interest? Doesn't seem likely."

"What's the position as regards the will?" my father asked. "Who actually gets old Leonides' money?"

Taverner heaved an exasperated sigh.

"You know what lawyers are. Can't get a straight answer out of them. There's a former will. Made when he married the second Mrs. Leonides. That leaves the same sum to her, rather less to Miss de Haviland, and the remainder between Philip and Roger. I should have thought that if this will isn't signed, then the old one would operate, but it seems it isn't so simple as that. First the making of the new will revoked the former one and there are witnesses to the signing of it, and the 'testator's intention.' It seems to be a toss-up if it turns out that he died intestate. Then the widow apparently gets the lot—or a life interest at any rate."

"So if the will's disappeared Brenda Leonides is the most likely person to profit by it?"

"Yes. If there's been any hocus-pocus, it seems probable that she's at the bottom of it. And there obviously *has* been hocus-pocus, but I'm dashed if I see how it was done."

I didn't see, either. I suppose we were really incredibly stupid. But we were looking at it, of course, from the wrong angle.

XII

THERE WAS a short silence after Taverner had gone out. Then I said:

"Dad, what are murderers like?"

The Old Man looked at me thoughtfully. We understand each other so well that he knew exactly what was in my mind when I put that question. And he answered it very seriously.

"Yes," he said. "That's important now—very important, for you . . . Murder's come close to you. You can't go on looking at it from the outside."

I had always been interested, in an amateurish kind of way, in some of the more spectacular "cases" with which the C.I.D. had dealt, but, as my father said, I had been interested from the outside—looking in, as it were, through the shop window. But now, as Sophia had seen much more quickly than I did, murder had become a dominant factor in my life.

The Old Man went on:

"I don't know if I'm the right person to ask. I could put you on to a couple of the tame psychiatrists who do jobs for us. They've got it all cut and dried. Or Taverner could give you all the inside dope. But you want, I take it, to hear what I, personally, as the result of my experience of criminals, think about it?"

"That's what I want," I said gratefully.

My father traced a little circle with his finger on the desk-top.

"What are murderers like? Some of them"—a faint rather melancholy smile showed on his face—"have been thoroughly nice chaps."

I think I looked a little startled.

"Oh yes, they have," he said. "Nice ordinary fellows like you and me—or like that chap who went out just now—Roger Leonides. Murder, you see, is an amateur crime. I'm speaking of course of the kind of murder you have in mind—not gangster stuff. One feels, very often, as though these nice ordinary chaps had been overtaken, as it were, by murder,

78

lmost accidentally. They've been in a tight place, or they've wanted something very badly, money or a woman—and they've killed to get it. The brake that operates with most of us doesn't operate with them. A child, you know, translates desire into action without compunction. A child is angry with its kitten, says 'I'll kill you,' and hits it on the head with a hammer—and then breaks its heart because the kitten doesn't come alive again! Lots of kids try to take a baby out of a pram and 'drown it,' because it usurps attention—or interferes with their pleasures. They get—very early—to a stage when they know that that is 'wrong'—that is, that it will be punished. Later, they get to *feel* that it is wrong. But some people, I suspect, remain morally immature. They continue to be aware that murder is wrong, but they do not feel it. I don't think, in my experience, that any murderer has really felt remorse. . . . And that, perhaps, is the mark of Cain. Murderers are set apart, they are 'different'—murder is wrong—but not for *them*—for them it is necessary—the victim has 'asked for it,' it was 'the only way.' "

"Do you think," I asked, "that if someone hated old Leonides, had hated him, say, for a very long time, that that would be a reason?"

"Pure hate? Very unlikely, I should say." My father looked at me curiously. "When you say hate, I presume you mean dislike carried to excess. A jealous hate is different—that rises out of affection and frustration. Constance Kent, everybody said, was very fond of the baby brother she killed. But she wanted, one supposes, the attention and the love that was bestowed on him. I think people more often kill those they love than those they hate. Possibly because only the people you love can really make life unendurable to you.

"But all this doesn't help you much, does it?" he went on. "What you want, if I read you correctly, is some token, some universal sign that will help you to pick out a murderer from a household of apparently normal and pleasant people?"

"Yes, that's it."

"Is there a common denominator? I wonder. You know," he paused in thought, "if there is, I should be inclined to say it is vanity."

"Vanity?"

"Yes, I've never met a murderer who wasn't vain. . . . It's their vanity that leads to their undoing, nine times out of

79

ten. They may be frightened of being caught, but they can help strutting and boasting and usually they're sure they've been far too clever to be caught." He added: "And here another thing, a murderer wants to *talk*."

"To talk?"

"Yes; you see, having committed a murder puts you in a position of great loneliness. You'd like to tell somebody all about it—and you never can. And that makes you want to all the more. And so—if you can't talk about how you did it, you can at least talk about the murder itself—discuss it advance theories—go over it.

"If I were you, Charles, I should look out for that. Go down there again, mix with them all, and get them to talk. Of course it won't be plain sailing. Guilty or innocent, they'll be glad of the chance to talk to a stranger, because they can say things to you that they couldn't say to each other. But it's possible, I think, that you might spot a difference. A person who has something to hide can't really afford to talk *at all*. The blokes knew that in Intelligence during the war. If you were captured, your name, rank, and number, but *nothing more*. People who attempt to give false information nearly always slip up. Get that household talking, Charles, and watch out for a slip or for some flash of self-revelation."

I told him then what Sophia had said about the ruthlessness in the family—the different kinds of ruthlessness. He was interested.

"Yes," he said. "Your young woman has got something there. Most families have got a defect, a chink in their armour. Most people can deal with one weakness—but they mightn't be able to deal with two weaknesses of a different kind. Interesting thing, heredity. Take the de Haviland ruthlessness, and what we might call the Leonides unscrupulousness—the de Havilands are all right because they're not unscrupulous, and the Leonides are all right because, though unscrupulous, they are kindly—but get a descendant who inherited both of those traits—see what I mean?"

I had not thought of it quite in those terms. My father said:

"But I shouldn't worry your head about heredity. It's much too tricky and complicated a subject. No, my boy, go down there and *let them talk to you*. Your Sophia is quite right about one thing. Nothing but the truth is going to be any good to her or to you. You've got to *know.*"

He added as I went out of the room:

"And be careful of the child."

"Josephine? You mean don't let on to her what I'm up to."

"No, I didn't mean that. I meant—look after her. We don't want anything to happen to her."

I stared at him.

"Come, come, Charles. There's a cold-blooded killer somewhere in that household. The child Josephine appears to know most of what goes on."

"She certainly knew all about Roger—even if she did leap to the conclusion that he was a swindler. Her account of what she overheard seems to have been quite accurate."

"Yes, yes. Child's evidence is always the best evidence there is. I'd rely on it every time. No good in court, of course. Children can't stand being asked direct questions. They mumble or else look idiotic and say they don't know. They're at their best when they're showing off. That's what the child was doing to you. Showing off. You'll get more out of her in the same way. Don't go asking her questions. Pretend you think she doesn't know anything. That'll fetch her."

He added:

"But take care of her. She may know a little too much for somebody's safety."

XIII

I went down to the Crooked House (as I called it in my own mind) with a slightly guilty feeling. Though I had repeated to Taverner Josephine's confidences about Roger, I had said nothing about her statement that Brenda and Laurence Brown wrote love letters to each other.

I excused myself by pretending that it was mere romancing, and that there was no reason to believe that it was true. But actually I had felt a strange reluctance to pile up additional evidence against Brenda Leonides. I had been affected by the pathos of her position in the house—surrounded by a hostile family united solidly against her. If such letters existed doubtless Taverner and his myrmidons would find them. I disliked to be the means of bringing fresh suspicion on a woman in a

81

difficult position. Moreover, she had assured me solemnly that there was nothing of that kind between her and Laurence and I felt more inclined to believe her than to believe that malicious gnome Josephine. Had not Brenda said herself that Josephine was "not all there"?

I stifled an uneasy certainty that Josephine was very much all there. I remembered the intelligence of her beady black eyes.

I had rung up Sophia and asked if I might come down again.

"Please do, Charles."

"How are things going?"

"I don't know. All right. They keep on searching the house. What are they looking for?"

"I've no idea."

"We're all getting very nervy. Come as soon as you can. I shall go crazy if I can't talk to someone."

I said I would come down straight away.

There was no one in sight as I drove up to the front door. I paid the taxi and it drove away. I felt uncertain whether to ring the bell or to walk in. The front door was open.

As I stood there, hesitating, I heard a slight sound behind me. I turned my head sharply. Josephine, her face partially obscured by a very large apple, was standing in the opening of the yew hedge looking at me.

As I turned my head, she turned away.

"Hallo, Josephine."

She did not answer, but disappeared behind the hedge. I crossed the drive and followed her. She was seated on the uncomfortable rustic bench by the goldfish pond swinging her legs to and fro and biting into her apple. Above its rosy circumference her eyes regarded me sombrely and with what I could not but feel was hostility.

"I've come down again, Josephine," I said.

It was a feeble opening, but I found Josephine's silence and her unblinking gaze rather unnerving.

With excellent strategic sense, she still did not reply.

"Is that a good apple?" I asked.

This time Josephine did condescend to reply. Her reply consisted of one word.

"Woolly."

"A pity," I said. "I don't like woolly apples."

Josephine replied scornfully:

82

"Nobody does."

"Why wouldn't you speak to me when I said hallo?"

"I didn't want to."

"Why not?"

Josephine removed the apple from her face to assist in the clearness of her denunciation.

"You went and sneaked to the police," she said.

"Oh!" I was rather taken aback. "You mean—about——"

"About Uncle Roger."

"But it's all right, Josephine," I asssured her. "Quite all right. They know he didn't do anything wrong—I mean, he hadn't embezzled any money or anything of that kind."

Josephine threw me an exasperated glance.

"How stupid you are."

"I'm sorry."

"I wasn't worrying about Uncle Roger. It's simply that that's not the way to do detective work. Don't you know that you *never* tell the police until the very end?"

"Oh, I see," I said. "I'm sorry, Josephine. I'm really very sorry."

"So you should be." She added reproachfully: "I trusted you."

I said I was sorry for the third time. Josephine appeared a little mollified. She took another couple of bites of apple.

"But the police would have been bound to find out about all this," I said. "You—I—we couldn't have kept it a secret."

"You mean because he's going bankrupt?"

As usual Josephine was well informed.

"I suppose it will come to that."

"They're going to talk about it to-night," said Josephine. "Father and Mother and Uncle Roger and Aunt Edith. Aunt Edith would give him her money—only she hasn't got it yet—but I don't think Father will. He says if Roger has got in a jam he's only got himself to blame and what's the good of throwing good money after bad, and Mother won't hear of giving him any because she wants Father to put up the money for Edith Thompson. Do you know about Edith Thompson? She was married, but she didn't like her husband. She was in love with a young man called Bywaters who came off a ship and he went down a different street after the theatre and stabbed him in the back."

I marvelled once more at the range and completeness of

Josephine's knowledge; and also at the dramatic sense which, only slightly obscured by hazy pronouns, had presented all the salient facts in a nutshell.

"It sounds all right," said Josephine, "but I don't suppose the play will be like that at all. It will be like *Jezebel* again." She sighed. "I wish I knew *why* the dogs wouldn't eat the palms of her hands."

"Josephine," I said. "You told me that you were almost sure who the murderer was?"

"Well?"

"Who is it?"

She gave me a look of scorn.

"I see," I said. "Not till the last chapter? Not even if I promise not to tell Inspector Taverner?"

"I want just a few more clues," said Josephine.

"Anyway," she added, throwing the core of the apple into the goldfish pool, "I wouldn't tell *you*. If you're anyone, you're Watson."

I stomached this insult.

"O.K.," I said. "I'm Watson. But even Watson was given the data."

"The what?"

"The facts. And then he made the wrong deductions from them. Wouldn't it be a lot of fun for you to see me making the wrong deductions?"

For a moment Josephine was tempted. Then she shook her head.

"No," she said, and added: "Anyway, I'm not very keen on Sherlock Holmes. It's awfully old-fashioned. They drive about in dog-carts."

"What about those letters?" I asked.

"What letters?"

"The letters you said Laurence Brown and Brenda wrote to each other."

"I made that up," said Josephine.

"I don't believe you."

"Yes, I did. I often make things up. It amuses me."

I stared at her. She stared back.

"Look here, Josephine. I know a man at the British Museum who knows a lot about the Bible. If I find out from him why the dogs didn't eat the palms of Jezebel's hands, will you tell me about those letters?"

This time Josephine really hesitated.

Somewhere, not very far away, a twig snapped with a sharp cracking noise. Josephine said flatly:

"No, I won't."

I accepted defeat. Rather late in the day, I remembered my father's advice.

"Oh well," I said, "it's only a game. Of course you don't really know anything."

Josephine's eyes snapped, but she resisted the bait.

I got up. "I must go in now," I said, "and find Sophia. Come along."

"I shall stop here," said Josephine.

"No, you won't," I said. "You're coming in with me."

Unceremoniously I yanked her to her feet. She seemed surprised and inclined to protest, but yielded with a fairly good grace—partly, no doubt, because she wished to observe the reactions of the household to my presence.

Why I was so anxious for her to accompany me I could not at that moment have said. It only came to me as we were passing through the front door.

It was because of the sudden snapping of a twig.

XIV

THERE WAS a murmur of voices from the big drawing-room. I hesitated but did not go in. I wandered down the passage and, led by some impulse, I pushed open a baize door. The passage beyond was dark, but suddenly a door opened showing a big lighted kitchen. In the doorway stood an old woman—a rather bulky old woman. She had a very clean white apron tied round her ample waist and the moment I saw her I knew that everything was all right. It is the feeling that a good Nannie can always give you. I am thirty-five, but I felt just like a reassured little boy of four.

As far as I knew, Nannie had never seen me, but she said at once:

"It's Mr. Charles, isn't it? Come into the kitchen and let me give you a cup of tea."

It was a big happy-feeling kitchen. I sat down by the centre table and Nannie brought me a cup of tea and two sweet biscuits on a plate. I felt more than ever that I was in the nursery again. Everything was all right—and the terrors of the dark and the unknown were no more with me.

"Miss Sophia will be glad you've come," said Nannie. "She's been getting rather over-excited." She added disapprovingly: "They're all over-excited."

I looked over my shoulder.

"Where's Josephine? She came in with me."

Nannie made a disapproving clacking noise with her tongue.

"Listening at doors and writing down things in that silly little book she carries about with her," she said. "She ought to have gone to school and had children of her own age to play with. I've said so to Miss Edith and she agrees—but the master would have it that she was best here in her home."

"I suppose he's very fond of her," I said.

"He was, sir. He was fond of them all."

I looked slightly astonished, wondering why Philip's affection for his offspring was put so definitely in the past. Nannie saw my expression and flushing slightly, she said:

"When I said the master, it was old Mr. Leonides I meant."

Before I could respond to that, the door opened with a rush and Sophia came in.

"Oh, Charles," she said, and then quickly: "Oh, Nannie, I'm so glad he's come."

"I know you are, love."

Nannie gathered up a lot of pots and pans and went off into a scullery with them. She shut the door behind her.

I got up from the table and went over to Sophia. I put my arms round her and held her to me.

"Dearest," I said. "You're trembling. What is it?"

Sopsia said:

"I'm frightened, Charles. I'm frightened."

"I love you," I said. "If I could take you away——"

She drew apart and shook her head.

"No, that's impossible. We've got to see this through. But you know, Charles, I don't like it. I don't like the feeling that someone—someone in this house—someone I see and speak to every day is a cold-blooded, calculating poisoner. . . ."

And I didn't know how to answer that. To someone like Sophia one can give no easy meaningless reassurances.

She said: "If only one *knew*——"

"That must be the worst of it," I agreed.

86

"You know what really frightens me?" she whispered. "It's that we may *never* know. . . ."

I could visualise easily what a nightmare that would be. . . . And it seemed to me highly probable that it never might be known who had killed old Leonides.

But it also reminded me of a question I had meant to put to Sophia on a point that had interested me.

"Tell me, Sophia," I said. "How many people in this house knew about the eserine eyedrops—I mean (a) that your grandfather had them, and (b) that they were poisonous and what would be a fatal dose?"

"I see what you're getting at, Charles. But it won't work. You see, we all knew."

"Well, yes, vaguely, I suppose, but specifically——"

"We knew specifically. We were all up with grandfather one day for coffee after lunch. He liked all the family round him, you know. And his eyes had been giving him a lot of trouble. And Brenda got the eserine to put a drop in each eye, and Josephine, who always asks questions about everything, said: 'Why does it say *"Eyedrops—not to be taken"* on the bottle?' And grandfather smiled and said: 'If Brenda were to make a mistake and inject eyedrops into me one day instead of insulin—I suspect I should give a big gasp, and go rather blue in the face and then die, because you see, my heart isn't very strong.' And Josephine said: 'Oo,' and grandfather went on: 'So we must be careful that Brenda does not give me an injection of eserine instead of insulin, mustn't we?' " Sophia paused and then said: "We were all there listening. You see? We all heard!"

I did see. I had some faint idea in my mind that just a little specialised knowledge would have been needed. But now it was borne in upon me that old Leonides had actually supplied the blue-print for his own murder. The murderer had not had to think out a scheme, or to plan or devise anything. A simple easy method of causing death had been supplied by the victim himself.

I drew a deep breath. Sophia, catching my thought, said: "Yes, it's rather horrible, isn't it?"

"You know, Sophia," I said slowly. "There's just one thing does strike me."

"Yes?"

"That you're right, and that it couldn't have been Brenda.

87

She couldn't do it exactly that way—when you'd all listened —when you'd all remember."

"I don't know about that. She is rather dumb in some ways, you know."

"Not as dumb as all that," I said. "No, it couldn't have been Brenda."

Sophia moved away from me.

"You don't want it to be Brenda, do you?" she asked.

And what could I say? I couldn't—no, I couldn't—say flatly: "Yes, I hope it *is* Brenda."

Why couldn't I? Just the feeling that Brenda was all alone on one side, and the concentrated animosity of the powerful Leonides family was arrayed against her on the other side? Chivalry? A feeling for the weaker? For the defenceless? I remembered her sitting on the sofa in her expensive rich mourning, the hopelessness in her voice—the fear in her eyes.

Nannie came back rather opportunely from the scullery. I don't know whether she sensed a certain strain between myself and Sophia.

She said disapprovingly:

"Talking murders and such-like. Forget about it, that's what I say. Leave it to the police. It's their nasty business, not yours."

"Oh, Nannie—don't you realise that someone in this house is a murderer——"

"Nonsense, Miss Sophia, I've no patience with you. Isn't the front door open all the time—all the doors open, nothing locked—asking for thieves and burglars?"

"But it couldn't have been a burglar, nothing was stolen. Besides, why should a burglar come in and poison somebody?"

"I didn't say it was a burglar, Miss Sophia. I only said all the doors were open. Anyone could have got in. If you ask me it was the Communists."

Nannie nodded her head in a satisfied way.

"Why on earth should Communists want to murder poor grandfather?"

"Well, everyone says that they're at the bottom of everything that goes on. But if it wasn't the Communists, mark my word, it was the Catholics. The Scarlet Woman of Babylon, that's what they are."

With the air of one saying the last word, Nannie disappeared again into the scullery.

Sophia and I laughed.

"A good old Black Protestant," I said.

"Yes, isn't she? Come on, Charles, come into the drawing-room. There's a kind of family conclave going on. It was scheduled for this evening—but it's started prematurely."

"I'd better not butt in, Sophia."

"If you're ever going to marry into the family, you'd better see just what it's like when it has the gloves off."

"What's it all about?"

"Roger's affairs. You seem to have been mixed up in them already. But you're crazy to think that Roger would ever have killed grandfather. Why, Roger adored him."

"I didn't really think Roger had. I thought Clemency might have."

"Only because I put it into your head. But you're wrong there too. I don't think Clemency will mind a bit if Roger loses all his money. I think she'll actually be rather pleased. She's got a queer kind of passion for *not* having things. Come on."

When Sophia and I entered the drawing-room, the voices that were speaking stopped abruptly. Everybody looked at us.

They were all there. Philip sitting in a big crimson brocaded arm-chair between the windows, his beautiful face set in a cold, stern mask. He looked like a judge about to pronounce sentence. Roger was astride a big pouffe by the fireplace. He had ruffled up his hair between his fingers until it stood up all over his head. His left trouser leg was rucked up and his tie was askew. He looked flushed and argumentative. Clemency sat beyond him, her slight form seemed too slender for the big stuffed chair. She was looking away from the others and seemed to be studying the wall panels with a dispassionate gaze. Edith sat in a grandfather chair, bolt upright. She was knitting with incredible energy, her lips pressed tightly together. The most beautiful thing in the room to look at was Magda and Eustace. They looked like a portrait by Gainsborough. They sat together on the sofa —the dark, handsome boy with a sullen expression on his face, and beside him, one arm thrust out along the back of the sofa, sat Magda, the Duchess of Three Gables in a picture gown of taffetas with one small foot in a brocaded slipper thrust out in front of her.

Philip frowned.

"Sophia," he said, "I'm sorry, but we are discussing family matters which are of a private nature."

Miss de Haviland's needles clicked. I prepared to apologise and retreat. Sophia forestalled me. Her voice was clear and determined.

"Charles and I," she said, "hope to get married. I want Charles to be here."

"And why on earth not?" cried Roger, springing up from his pouffe with explosive energy. "I keep telling you, Philip there's nothing *private* about this! The whole world is going to know to-morrow or the day after. Anyway, my dear boy," he came and put a friendly hand on my shoulder "*you* know all about it. You were there this morning."

"Do tell me," cried Magda, leaning forward. "What is it like at Scotland Yard? One always wonders. A table? A desk? Chairs? What kind of curtains? No flowers, I suppose? A dictaphone?"

"Put a sock in it, Mother," said Sophia. "And anyway, you told Vavasour Jones to cut that Scotland Yard scene. You said it was an anti-climax."

"It makes it too like a detective play," said Magda. "Edith Thompson is definitely a psychological drama—or psychological thriller—which do you think sounds best?"

"You were there this morning?" Philip asked me sharply. "Why? Oh, of course—your father——"

He frowned. I realised more clearly than ever that my presence was unwelcome, but Sophia's hand was clenched on my arm.

Clemency moved a chair forward.

"Do sit down," she said.

I gave her a grateful glance and accepted.

"You may say what you like," said Miss de Haviland, apparently going on from where they had all left off, "but I do think we ought to respect Aristide's wishes. When this will business is straightened out, as far as I am concerned, my legacy is entirely at your disposal, Roger."

Roger tugged his hair in a frenzy.

"No Aunt Edith. *No!*" he cried.

"I wish I could say the same," said Philip, "but one has to take every factor into consideration——"

"Dear old Phil, don't you understand? I'm not going to take a penny from *anyone*."

"Of course he can't!" snapped Clemency.

"Anyway, Edith," said Magda. "*If* the will is straightened out, he'll have his own legacy."

"But it can't possibly be straightened out in time, can it?" asked Eustace.

"You don't know anything about it, Eustace," said Philip.

"The boy's absolutely right," cried Roger. "He's put his finger on the spot. Nothing can avert the crash. Nothing."

He spoke with a kind of relish.

"There is really nothing to discuss," said Clemency.

"Anyway," said Roger, "what does it matter?"

"I should have thought it mattered a good deal," said Philip, pressing his lips together.

"No," said Roger. "*No!* Does anything matter compared with the fact that father is dead? Father is *dead!* And we sit here discussing mere money matters!"

A faint colour rose in Philip's pale cheeks.

"We are only trying to help," he said stiffly.

"I know, Phil, old boy, I know. But there's nothing anyone can do. So let's call it a day."

"I suppose," said Philip, "that I *could* raise a certain amount of money. Securities have gone down a good deal and some of my capital is tied up in such a way that I can't touch it: Magda's settlement and so on—but——"

Magda said quickly:

"Of course you can't raise the money, darling. It would be absurd to try—and not very fair on the children."

"I tell you I'm not asking anyone for *anything!*" shouted Roger. "I'm *hoarse* with telling you so. I'm quite content that things should take their course."

"It's a question of prestige," said Philip. "Father's. Ours."

"It wasn't a family business. It was solely *my* concern."

"Yes," said Philip, looking at him. "It was entirely your concern."

Edith de Haviland got up and said: "I think we've discussed this enough."

There was in her voice that authentic note of authority that never fails to produce its effect.

Philip and Magda got up. Eustace lounged out of the room and I noticed the stiffness of his gait. He was not exactly lame, but his walk was a halting one.

Roger linked his arm in Philip's and said:

"You've been a brick, Phil, even to think of such a thing!" The brothers went out together.

Magda murmured, "Such a fuss!" as she followed them, and Sophia said that she must see about my room.

Edith de Haviland stood rolling up her knitting. She looked towards me and I thought she was going to speak to me. There was something almost like appeal in her glance. However, she changed her mind, sighed, and went out after the others.

Clemency had moved over to the window and stood looking out into the garden. I went over and stood beside her. She turned her head slightly towards me.

"Thank goodness that's over," she said—and added with distaste: "What a preposterous room this is!"

"Don't you like it?"

"I can't breathe in it. There's always a smell of half-dead flowers and dust."

I thought she was unjust to the room. But I knew what she meant. It was very definitely an interior.

It was a woman's room, exotic, soft, shut away from the rude blasts of outside weather. It was not a room that a man would be happy in for long. It was not a room where you could relax and read the newspaper and smoke a pipe and put up your feet. Nevertheless I preferred it to Clemency's own abstract expression of herself upstairs. On the whole I prefer a boudoir to an operating theatre.

She said, looking round:

"It's just a stage set. A background for Magda to play her scenes against." She looked at me. "You realise, don't you, what we've just been doing? Act II—the family conclave. Magda arranged it. It didn't mean a thing. There was nothing to talk about, nothing to discuss. It's all settled—finished."

There was no sadness in her voice. Rather there was satisfaction. She caught my glance.

"Oh, don't you understand?" she said impatiently. "We're *free*—at last! Don't you understand that Roger's been miserable—absolutely *miserable*—for years? He never had any aptitude for business. He likes things like horses and cows and pottering round in the country. But he adored his father —they all did. That's what's wrong with this house—too much family. I don't mean that the old man was a tyrant, or reyed upon them, or bullied them. He didn't. He gave them money and freedom. He was devoted to them. And they kept on being devoted to him."

"Is there anything wrong in that?"

"I think there is. I think, when your children have grown up, that you should cut away from them, efface yourself, slink away, *force* them to forget you."

"Force them? That's rather drastic, isn't it? Isn't coercion as bad one way as another?"

"If he hadn't made himself such a personality——"

"You can't make yourself a personality," I said. "He *was* a personality."

"He was too much of a personality for Roger. Roger worshipped him. He wanted to do everything his father wanted him to do, he wanted to be the kind of son his father wanted. And he couldn't. His father made over Associated Catering to him—it was the old man's particular joy and pride, and Roger tried hard to carry on in his father's footsteps. But he hadn't got that kind of ability. In business matters Roger is—yes, I'll say it plainly—a fool. And it nearly broke his heart. He's been miserable for years, struggling, seeing the whole thing go down the hill, having sudden wonderful 'ideas' and 'schemes' which always went wrong and made it worse than ever. It's a terrible thing to feel you're a failure year after year. You don't know how unhappy he's been. I do."

Again she turned and faced me.

"You thought, you actually suggested to the police, that Roger would have killed his father—for money! You don't know how—how absolutely *ricidulous* that is!"

"I do know it now," I said humbly.

"When Roger knew he couldn't stave it off any more—that the crash was bound to come, he was actually relieved. Yes, he was. He worried about his father's knowing—but not about anything else. He was looking forward to the new life we were going to live."

Her face quivered a little and her voice softened.

"Where were you going?" I asked.

"To Barbados. A distant cousin of mine died a short time ago and left me a tiny estate out there—oh, nothing much. But it was somewhere to go. We'd have been desperately poor, but we'd have scratched a living—it costs very little just to live. We'd have been together—unworried, away from them all."

She sighed.

"Roger is a ridiculous person. He would worry about *me*—about *my* being poor. I suppose he's got the Leonides' attitude to money too firmly in his mind. When my first husband was alive, we were terribly poor—and Roger thinks it was so brave and wonderful of me! He doesn't realise that I was *happy*—really happy! I've never been so happy since. And yet—I never loved Richard as I love Roger."

Her eyes half-closed. I was aware of the intensity of her feeling.

She opened her eyes, looked at me and said:

"So you see, I would never have killed anyone for money. I don't *like* money."

I was quite sure that she meant exactly what she said. Clemency Leonides was one of those rare people to whom money does not appeal. They dislike luxury, prefer austerity and are suspicious of possessions.

Still, there are many to whom money has no personal appeal, but who can be tempted by the power it confers.

I said: "You mightn't want money for yourself—but wisely directed, money can do a lot of interesting things. It can endow research, for example."

I had suspected that Clemency might be a fanatic about her work, but she merely said:

"I doubt if endowments ever do much good. They're usually spent in the wrong way. The things that are worth while are usually accomplished by someone with enthusiasm and drive—and with natural vision. Expensive equipment and training and experiment never does what you'd imagine it might do. The spending of it usually gets into the wrong hands."

"Will you mind giving up your work when you go to Barbados?" I asked. "You're still going, I presume?"

"Oh, yes, as soon as the police will let us. No, I shan't mind giving up my work at all. Why should I? I wouldn't like to be idle, but I shan't be idle in Barbados."

She added impatiently:

"Oh, if only this could all be cleared up *quickly* and we could get away."

"Clemency," I said, "have you any idea at all who did

o this? Granting that you and Roger had no hand in it (and really I can't see any reason to think you had), surely, with our intelligence, you must have *some* idea of who did?"

She gave me a rather peculiar look, a darting, sideways glance. When she spoke her voice had lost its spontaneity. It was awkward, rather embarrassed.

"One can't make guesses, it's unscientific," she said. "One can only say that Brenda and Laurence are the obvious suspects."

"So you think they did it?"

Clemency shrugged her shoulders.

She stood for a moment as though listening, then she went out of the room, passing Edith de Haviland in the doorway.

Edith came straight over to me.

"I want to talk to you," she said.

My father's words leapt into my mind. Was this——

But Edith de Haviland was going on:

"I hope you didn't get the wrong impression," she said. "About Philip, I mean. Philip is rather difficult to understand. He may seem to you reserved and cold, but that is not so at all. It's just a manner. He can't help it."

"I really hadn't thought——" I began.

But she swept on:

"Just now—about Roger. It isn't really that he's grudging. He's never been mean about money. And he's really a dear —he's always been a dear—but he needs understanding."

I looked at her with the air, I hope, of one who was willing to understand. She went on:

"It's partly, I think, from having been the second of the family. There's often something about a second child—they start handicapped. He adored his father. Of course, all the children adored Aristide and he adored them. But Roger was his especial pride and joy. Being the eldest—the first. And I think Philip felt it. He drew back right into himself. He began to like books and the past and things that were well divorced from everyday life. I think he suffered—children do suffer . . ."

She paused and went on:

"What I really mean, I suppose, is that he's always been jealous of Roger. I think perhaps he doesn't know it himself. But I think the fact that Roger has come a cropper—oh, it seems an odious thing to say and really I'm sure he doesn't

realise it himself—but I think perhaps Philip isn't as sorr
about it as he ought to be."

"You mean really that he's rather pleased Roger has mad
a fool of himself."

"Yes," said Miss de Haviland. "I mean just exactly that."

She added, frowning a little:

"It distressed me, you know, that he didn't at once offe
to help his brother."

"Why should he?" I said. "After all, Roger *has* made
muck of things. He's a grown man. There are no children t
consider. If he were ill or in real want, of course his family
would help—but I've no doubt Roger would really much
prefer to start afresh entirely on his own."

"Oh! he would. It's only Clemency he minds about. An
Clemency is an extraordinary creature. She really likes being
uncomfortable and having only one utility tea-cup to drink
out of. Modern, I suppose. She's no sense of the past, no
sense of beauty."

I felt her shrewd eyes looking me up and down.

"This is a dreadful ordeal for Sophia," she said. "I am
so sorry her youth should be dimmed by it. I love them all
you know. Roger and Philip, and now Sophia and Eustace
and Josephine. All the dear children. Marcia's children. Yes,
I love them dearly." She paused and then added sharply:
"But, mind you, this side idolatry."

She turned abruptly and went. I had the feeling that she had
meant something by her last remark that I did not quite
understand.

XV

"Your room's ready," said Sophia.

She stood by my side looking out at the garden. It looked
bleak and grey now with the half-denuded trees swaying in
the wind.

Sophia echoed my thoughts as she said:

"How desolate it looks . . ."

As we watched, a figure, and then presently another came
through the yew hedge from the rock garden. They both
looked grey and unsubstantial in the fading light.

Brenda Leonides was the first. She was wrapped in a grey
chinchilla coat and there was something catlike and stealthy

in the way she moved. She slipped through the twilight with a kind of eerie grace.

I saw her face as she passed the window. There was a half-smile on it, the curving, crooked smile I had noticed upstairs. A few minutes later Laurence Brown, looking slender and shrunken, also slipped through the twilight. I can only put it that way. They did not seem like two people walking, two people who had been out for a stroll. There was something furtive and unsubstantial about them like two ghosts.

I wondered if it was under Brenda's or Laurence's foot a twig had snapped.

By a natural association of ideas, I asked:

"Where's Josephine?"

"Probably with Eustace up in the schoolroom." She frowned. "I'm worried about Eustace, Charles."

"Why?"

"He's so moody and odd. He's been so different ever since that wretched paralysis. I can't make out what's going on in his mind. Sometimes he seems to hate us all."

"He'll probably grow out of all that. It's just a phase."

"Yes, I suppose so. But I do get worried, Charles."

"Why, dear heart?"

"Really, I suppose, because mother and father never worry. They're not like a mother and father."

"That may be all for the best. More children suffer from interference than from non-interference."

"That's true. You know, I never thought about it until I came back from abroad, but they really are a queer couple. Father living determinedly in a world of obscure historical by-paths and mother having a lovely time creating scenes. That tomfoolery this evening was all mother. There was no need for it. She just wanted to play a family conclave scene. She gets bored, you know, down here and has to try and work up a drama."

For the moment I had a fantastic vision of Sophia's mother poisoning her elderly father-in-law in a light-hearted manner in order to observe a murder drama at first-hand with herself in the leading role.

An amusing thought! I dismissed it as such—but it left me a little uneasy.

"Mother," said Sophia, "has to be looked after the whole time. You never know *what* she's up to!"

"Forget your family, Sophia," I said firmly.

"I shall be only too delighted to, but it's a little difficult at the present moment. But I *was* happy out in Cairo when I had forgotten them all."

I remembered how Sophia had never mentioned her home or her people.

"Is that why you never talked about them?" I asked. "Because you wanted to forget them?"

"I think so. We've always, all of us, lived too much in each other's pockets. We're—we're all too fond of each other. We're not like some families where they all hate each other like poison. That must be pretty bad, but it's almost worse to live all tangled up in conflicting affections."

She added:

"I think that's what I mean when I said we all lived together in a little crooked house. I didn't mean that it was crooked in the dishonest sense. I think what I meant was that we hadn't been able to grow up independent, standing by ourselves, upright. We're all a bit twisted and twining."

I saw Edith de Haviland's heel grinding a weed into the path as Sophia added:

"Like bindweed . . ."

And then suddenly Magda was with us—flinging open the door—crying out:

"Darlings, why don't you have the lights on? It's almost dark."

And she pressed the switches and the lights sprang up on the walls and on the tables, and she and Sophia and I pulled the heavy rose curtains, and there we were in the flower-scented interior, and Magda, flinging herself on the sofa, cried:

"What an incredible scene it was, wasn't it? How cross Eustace was! He told me he thought it was all positively indecent. How funny boys are!"

She sighed.

"Roger's rather a pet. I love him when he rumples his hair and starts knocking things over. Wasn't it sweet of Edith to offer her legacy to him? She really meant it, you know, it wasn't just a gesture. But it was terribly stupid—it might have made Philip think he ought to do it too! Of course Edith would do *anything* for the family! There's something very pathetic in the love of a spinster for her sister's children.

me day I shall play one of those devoted spinster aunts. quisitive and obstinate and devoted."

"It must have been hard for her after her sister died," I d, refusing to be side-tracked into discussion of another of agda's roles. "I mean if she disliked old Leonides so much." Magda interrupted me.

"Disliked him? Who told you that? Nonsense. She was in ve with him."

"Mother!" said Sophia.

"Now don't try and contradict me, Sophia. Naturally at ur age, you think love is all two good-looking young people the moonlight."

"She told me," I said, "that she had always disliked him."

"Probably she did when she first came. She'd been angry th her sister for marrying him. I dare say there was always me antagonism—but she was in love with him all right! arling, I do know what I'm talking about! Of course, with ceased wife's sister and all that, he couldn't have married r, and I dare say he never thought of it—and quite probably e didn't either. She was quite happy mothering the children, d having fights with him. But she didn't like it when he arried Brenda. She didn't like it a *bit*!"

"No more did you and father," said Sophia.

"No, of course we hated it! Naturally! But Edith hated it ost. Darling, the way I've seen her *look* at Brenda!"

"Now, Mother," said Sophia.

Magda threw her an affectionate and half-guilty glance, the ance of a mischievous, spoilt child.

She went on, with no apparent realisation of any lack of ntinuity:

"I've decided Josephine really must go to school."

"Josephine? To school?"

"Yes. To Switzerland. I'm going to see about it to- orrow. I really think we might get her off *at once*. It's so d for her to be mixed up in a horrid business like this. She's tting quite morbid about it. What she needs is other ildren of her own age. School life. I've always thought so."

"Grandfather didn't want her to go to school," said Sophia owly. "He was very much against it."

"Darling old Sweetie Pie liked us all here under his eye. ery old people are often selfish in that way. A child ought be amongst other children. And Switzerland is so healthy

99

—all the winter sports, and the air, and so much, much bett
food than we get here!"

"It will be difficult to arrange for Switzerland now wi
all the currency regulations, won't it?" I asked.

"Nonsense, Charles. There's some kind of education
racket—or you exchange with a Swiss child—there are a
sorts of ways. Rudolph Alstir's in Lausanne. I shall wire hi
to-morrow to arrange *everything*. We can get her off by t
end of the week!"

Magda punched a cushion, smiled at us, went to the doo
stood a moment looking back at us in a quite enchantir
fashion.

"It's only the young who count," she said. As she said it,
was a lovely line. "They must always come first. And, darlin
—think of the flowers—the blue gentians, the narcissus . .

"In October?" asked Sophia, but Magda had gone.

Sophia heaved an exasperated sigh.

"Really," she said. "Mother is too trying! She gets the
sudden ideas, and she sends thousands of telegrams an
everything has to be arranged at a moment's notice. Wh
should Josephine be hustled off to Switzerland all in a flurry?

"There's probably something in the idea of school. I thin
children of her own age would be a good thing for Josephine.

"Grandfather didn't think so," said Sophia obstinately.

I felt slightly irritated.

"My dear Sophia, do you really think an old gentlema
of over eighty is the best judge of a child's welfare?"

"He was about the best judge of anybody in this house,
said Sophia.

"Better than your Aunt Edith?"

"No, perhaps not. She did rather favour school. I admi
Josephine's got into rather difficult ways—she's got a horribl
habit of snooping. But I really think it's just because she
playing detectives."

Was it only the concern for Josephine's welfare which ha
occasioned Magda's sudden decision? I wondered. Josephin
was remarkably well-informed about all sorts of things tha
had happened prior to the murder and which had been cer
tainly no business of hers. A healthy school life with plent
of games would probably do her a world of good. But I di
rather wonder at the suddenness and urgency of Magda'
decision—Switzerland was a long way off.

100

XVI

The Old Man had said:

"Let them talk to you."

As I shaved the following morning, I considered just how far that had taken me.

Edith de Haviland had talked to me—she had sought me out for that especial purpose. Clemency had talked to me (or had I talked to her?). Magda had talked to me in a sense—that is, I had formed part of the audience to one of her broadcasts. Sophia naturally had talked to me. Even Nannie had talked to me. Was I any the wiser for what I had learned from them all? Was there any significant word or phrase? More, was there any evidence of that abnormal vanity on which my father had laid stress? I couldn't see that there was. The only person who had shown absolutely no desire to talk to me in any way, or on any subject, was Philip. Was not that, in a way, rather abnormal? He must know by now that I wanted to marry his daughter. Yet he continued to act as though I was not in the house at all. Presumably he resented my presence there. Edith de Haviland had apologised for him. She had said it was just "manner." She had shown herself concerned about Philip. Why?

I considered Sophia's father. He was in every sense a repressed individual. He had been an unhappy jealous child. He had been forced back into himself. He had taken refuge in the world of books—in the historical past. That studied coldness and reserve of his might conceal a good deal of passionate feeling. The inadequate motive of financial gain by his father's death was unconvincing—I did not think for a moment that Philip Leonides would kill his father because he himself had not quite as much money as he would like to have. But there might be some deep psychological reason for his desiring his father's death. Philip had come back to his father's house to live, and later, as a result of the Blitz, Roger had come—and Philip had been obliged to see day by day that Roger was his father's favourite . . . Might things have come to such a pass in his tortured mind that the only relief possible was his father's death? And supposing that death should incriminate his elder brother? Roger was short of money—on the verge of a crash. Knowing nothing of that last interview between Roger and his father and the latter's offer of assistance, might not Philip have believed that the motive would seem so powerful that Roger would be at once suspected? Was Philip's mental balance sufficiently disturbed to lead him to do murder?

I cut my chin with the razor and swore.

What the hell was I trying to do? Fasten murder on Sophia's father? That was a nice thing to try and do! That wasn't what Sophia had wanted me to come down here for.

Or—was it? There was something, had been something all along, behind Sophia's appeal. If there was any lingering suspicion in her mind that her father was the killer, then she would never consent to marry me—in case that suspicion might be true. And since she was Sophia, clear-eyed and brave, she wanted the truth, since uncertainty would be an eternal and perpetual barrier between us. Hadn't she been in effect saying to me, "Prove that this dreadful thing I am imagining is not true—but if it *is* true, then prove its truth to me—so that I can know the worst and face it!"

Did Edith de Haviland know, or suspect, that Philip was guilty. What had she meant by "this side idolatry?"

And what had Clemency meant by that peculiar look she had thrown at me when I had asked her who she suspected and she had answered: "Laurence and Brenda are the obvious suspects, aren't they?"

The whole family wanted it to be Brenda and Laurence, hoped it might be Brenda and Laurence, but didn't really believe it was Brenda and Laurence . . .

And of course, the whole family might be wrong, and it might really be Laurence and Brenda after all.

Or, it might be Laurence, and not Brenda . . .

That would be a much better solution.

I finished dabbing my cut chin and went down to breakfast filled with the determination to have an interview with Laurence Brown as soon as possible.

It was only as I drank my second cup of coffee that it occurred to me that the Crooked House was having its effect on me also. I, too, wanted to find, not the true solution, but the solution that suited *me* best.

After breakfast I went through the hall and up the stairs. Sophia had told me that I should find Laurence giving instruction to Eustace and Josephine in the schoolroom.

I hesitated on the landing outside Brenda's front door. Did I ring and knock, or did I walk right in? I decided to treat the house as an integral Leonides home and not as Brenda's private residence.

I opened the door and passed inside. Everything was quiet, there seemed no one about. On my left the door into the big drawing-room was closed. On my right two open doors showed a bedroom and adjoining bathroom. This I knew was the bathroom adjoining Aristide Leonides' bedroom where the eserine and the insulin had been kept.

The police had finished with it now. I pushed the door open and slipped inside. I realised then how easy it would have been for anyone in the house (or from outside the house for the matter of that!) to come up here and into the bathroom unseen.

I stood in the bathroom looking round. It was sumptuously appointed with gleaming tiles and a sunk bath. At one side were various electric appliances; a hot plate and grill under, an electric kettle—a small electric saucepan, a toaster—everything that a valet attendant to an old gentleman might need. On the wall was a white enamelled cupboard. I opened it. Inside were medical appliances, two medicine glasses, eyebath, eye dropper, and a few labelled bottles. Aspirin, boracic powder, iodine. Elastoplast bandages, etc. On a separate shelf were the stacked supply of insulin, two hypodermic needles, and a bottle of surgical spirit. On a third shelf was a bottle marked The Tablets—one or two to be taken at night as ordered. On this shelf, no doubt, had stood the bottle of eyedrops. It was all clear, well arranged, easy for anyone to get at if needed, and equally easy to get at for murder.

I could do what I liked with the bottles and then go softly out and downstairs again and nobody would ever know I had been there. All this was, of course, nothing new, but it brought home to me how difficult the task of the police was.

Only from the guilty party or parties could one find out what one needed.

"Rattle 'em," Taverner had said to me. "Get 'em on the run. Make 'em think we're on to something. Keep ourselves well in the limelight. Sooner or later, if we do, our criminal will stop leaving well alone and try to be smarter still—and then—we've got him."

Well, the criminal hadn't reacted to this treatment so far.

I came out of the bathroom. Still no one about. I went on along the corridor. I passed the dining-room on the left, and Brenda's bedroom and bathroom on the right. In the latter, one of the maids was moving about. The dining-room door was closed. From a room beyond that, I heard Edith de Haviland's voice telephoning to the inevitable fishmonger. A spiral flight of stairs led to the floor above. I went up them. Edith's bedroom and sitting-room were here, I knew, and two more bathrooms and Laurence Brown's room. Beyond that again the short flight of steps down to the big room built out over the servants' quarters at the back which was used as a schoolroom.

Outside the door I paused. Laurence Brown's voice could be heard, slightly raised, from inside.

I think Josephine's habit of snooping must have been catching. Quite unashamedly I leaned against the door jamb and listened.

It was a history lesson that was in progress, and the period in question was the French *Directoire*.

As I listened astonishment opened my eyes. It was a considerable surprise to me to discover that Laurence Brown was a magnificent teacher.

I don't know why it should have surprised me so much. After all, Aristide Leonides had always been a good picker of men. For all his mouselike exterior, Laurence had that supreme gift of being able to rouse enthusiasm and imagination in his pupils. The drama of Thermidor, the decree of outlawry against the Robespierrists, the magnificence of Barras, the cunning of Fouché—Napoleon the half-starved young gunner lieutenant—all these were real and living.

Suddenly Laurence stopped, he asked Eustace and Josephine a question, he made them put themselves in the place of first one and then another figure in the drama. Though he didn't get much result from Josephine, whose voice sounded as though she had a cold in the head, Eustace sounded quite different from his usual moody self. He showed brains and intelligence and the keen historical sense which he had doubtless inherited from his father.

Then I heard the chairs being pushed back and scraped across the floor. I retreated up the steps and was apparently just coming down them when the door opened.

Eustace and Josephine came out.

"Hallo," I said.

Eustace looked surprised to see me.

"Do you want anything?" he asked politely.

Josephine, taking no interest in my presence, slipped past me.

"I just wanted to see the schoolroom," I said rather feebly.

"You saw it the other day, didn't you? It's just a kid's place really. Used to be the nursery. It's still got a lot of toys in it."

He held open the door for me and I went in.

Laurence Brown stood by the table. He looked up, flushed, murmured something in answer to my good morning and went hurriedly out.

"You've scared him," said Eustace. "He's very easily scared."

"Do you like him, Eustace?"

"Oh! he's all right. An awful ass, of course."

"But not a bad teacher?"

"No, as a matter of fact he's quite interesting. He knows an awful lot. He makes you see things from a different angle. I never knew that Henry the Eighth wrote poetry —to Ann Boleyn, of course—jolly decent poetry."

We talked for a few moments on such subjects as *The Ancient Mariner*, Chaucer, the political implications behind the Crusades, the medieval approach to life, and the, to Eustace, surprising fact that Oliver Cromwell had prohibited the celebration of Christmas Day. Behind Eustace's scornful and rather ill-tempered manner there was, I perceived, an inquiring and able mind.

Very soon, I began to realise the source of his ill humour. His illness had not only been a frightening ordeal, it had also been a frustration and a setback, just at a moment when he had been enjoying life.

"I was to have been in the eleven next term—and I'd got my house colours. It's pretty thick to have to stop at home and do lessons with a rotten kid like Josephine. Why, she's only twelve."

"Yes, but you don't have the same studies, do you?"

"No, of course she doesn't do advanced maths—or Latin. But you don't want to have to share a tutor with a *girl*."

I tried to soothe his injured male pride by remarking that Josephine was quite an intelligent girl for her age.

"D'you think so? I think she's awfully wet. She's mad keen on this detecting stuff—goes round poking her nose in every where and writing things down in a little black book an pretending that she's finding out a lot. Just a silly kid, that all she is," said Eustace loftily.

"Anyway," he added, "girls can't be detectives. I told he so. I think mother's quite right and the sooner Jo's packe off to Switzerland the better."

"Wouldn't you miss her?"

"Miss a kid of that age?" said Eustace haughtily. "O course not. My goodness, this house is the absolute limit Mother always haring up and down to London and bullyin, tame dramatists to rewrite plays for her, and making frightfu fusses about nothing at all. And father shut up with his book and sometimes not hearing you if you speak to him. I don' see why I should have to be burdened with such peculia: parents. Then there's Uncle Roger—always so hearty tha it makes you shudder. Aunt Clemency's all right, she doesn' bother you, but I sometimes think she's a bit batty. Aun Edith's not too bad, but she's old. Things have been a bi more cheerful since Sophia came back—though she can be pretty sharp sometimes. But it is a queer household, don' you think so? Having a step-grandmother young enough tc be your aunt or your older sister. I mean, it makes you feel an awful ass!"

I had some comprehension of his feelings. I remembered (very dimly) my own supersensitiveness at Eustace's age. My horror of appearing in any way unusual or of my near relatives departing from the normal.

"What about your grandfather?" I said. "Were you fond of him?"

A curious expression flitted across Eustace's face.

"Grandfather," he said, "was definitely anti-social!"

"In what way?"

"He thought of nothing but the profit motive. Laurence says that's completely wrong. And he was a great individualist. All that sort of thing has got to go, don't you think so?"

"Well," I said, rather brutally, "he has gone."

"A good thing, really," said Eustace. "I don't want to be callous, but you can't really *enjoy* life at that age!"

"Didn't he?"

"He couldn't have. Anyway, it was time he went. He——"

Eustace broke off as Laurence Brown came back into the schoolroom.

Laurence began fussing about with some books, but I thought that he was watching me out of the corner of his eye.

He looked at his wrist-watch and said:

"Please be back here sharp at eleven, Eustace. We've wasted too much time the last few days."

"O.K., sir."

Eustace lounged towards the door and went out whistling.

Laurence Brown darted another sharp glance at me. He moistened his lips once or twice. I was convinced that he had come back into the schoolroom solely in order to talk to me.

Presently, after a little aimless stacking and unstacking of books and a pretence of looking for a book that was missing, he spoke:

"Er—How are they getting on?" he said.

"They?"

"The police."

His nose twitched. A mouse in a trap, I thought, a mouse in a trap.

"They don't take me into their confidence," I said.

"Oh. I thought your father was the Assistant Commissioner."

"He is," I said. "But naturally he would not betray official secrets."

I made my voice purposely pompous.

"Then you don't know how—what—if——" His voice trailed off. "They're not going to make an arrest, are they?"

"Not so far as I know. But then, as I say, I mightn't know."

Get 'em on the run, Inspector Taverner had said. Get 'em rattled. Well, Laurence Brown was rattled all right.

He began talking quickly and nervously.

"You don't know what it's like . . . The strain . . . Not knowing what—I mean, they just come and go—Asking questions . . . Questions that don't seem to have anything to do with the case . . ."

He broke off. I waited. He wanted to talk—well, then, let him talk.

"You were there when the Chief Inspector made that monstrous suggestion the other day? About Mrs. Leonides and myself . . . It *was* monstrous. It makes one feel so helpless. One is powerless to prevent people *thinking* things!

107

And it is all so wickedly untrue. Just because she is—was—so many years younger than her husband. People have dreadful minds—dreadful minds. I feel—I can't help feeling, that it is all a *plot*."

"A plot? That's interesting."

It was interesting, though not quite in the way he took it.

"The family, you know; Mr. Leonides' family, have never been sympathetic to me. They were always aloof. I always felt that they despised me."

His hands had begun to shake.

"Just because they have always been rich and—powerful. They looked down on me. What was I to them? Only the tutor. Only a wretched conscientious objector. And my objections *were* conscientious. They were indeed!"

I said nothing.

"All right then," he burst out. "What if I was—afraid? Afraid I'd make a mess of it. Afraid that when I had to pull a trigger—I mightn't be able to bring myself to do it. How can you be sure it's a Nazi you're going to kill? It might be some decent lad—some village boy—with no political leanings, just called up for his country's service. I believe war is *wrong*, do you understand? I believe it is *wrong*."

I was still silent. I believed that my silence was achieving more than any arguments or agreements could do. Laurence Brown was arguing with himself, and in so doing was revealing a good deal of himself.

"Everyone's always laughed at me." His voice shook. "I seem to have a knack of making myself ridiculous. It isn't that I really lack courage—but I always do the thing wrong. I went into a burning house to rescue a woman they said was trapped there. But I lost the way at once, and the smoke made me unconscious, and it gave a lot of trouble to the firemen finding me. I heard them say, 'Why couldn't the silly chump leave it to us?' It's no good my trying, everyone's against me. Whoever killed Mr. Leonides arranged it so that I would be suspected. Someone killed him so as to ruin *me*."

"What about Mrs. Leonides?" I asked.

He flushed. He became less of a mouse and more like a man.

"Mrs. Leonides is an angel," he said, "an angel. Her sweetness, her kindness to her elderly husband were wonderful. To think of her in connection with poison is laughable —laughable! And that thick-headed Inspector can't see it!"

"He's prejudiced," I said, "by the number of cases on his files where elderly husbands have been poisoned by sweet young wives."

"The insufferable dolt," said Laurence Brown angrily.

He went over to a bookcase in the corner and began rummaging the books in it. I didn't think I should get anything more out of him. I went slowly out of the room.

As I was going along the passage, a door on my left opened and Josephine almost fell on top of me. Her appearance had the suddenness of a demon in an old-fashioned pantomime.

Her face and hands were filthy and a large cobweb floated from one ear.

"Where have you been, Josephine?"

I peered through the half-open door. A couple of steps led up into an attic-like rectangular space in the gloom of which several large tanks could be seen.

"In the cistern room."

"Why in the cistern room?"

Josephine replied in a brief businesslike way:

"Detecting."

"What on earth is there to detect among the cisterns?"

To this, Josephine merely replied:

"I must wash."

"I should say most decidedly."

Josephine disappeared through the nearest bathroom door. She looked back to say:

"I should say it's about time for the next murder, wouldn't you?"

"What do you mean—the next murder?"

"Well, in books there's always a second murder about now. Someone who knows something is bumped off before they can tell what they know."

"You read too many detective stories, Josephine. Real life isn't like that. And if anybody in this house knows something the last thing they seem to want to do is to talk about it."

Josephine's reply came to me rather obscurely by the gushing of water from a tap.

"Sometimes it's something that they don't know that they do know."

I blinked as I tried to think this out. Then, leaving Josephine to her ablutions, I went down to the floor below.

Just as I was going out through the front door to the
109

staircase, Brenda came with a soft rush through the drawing-room door.

She came close to me and laid her hand on my arm, looking up in my face.

"Well?" she asked.

It was the same demand for information that Laurence had made, only it was phrased differently. And her one word was far more effective.

I shook my head.

"Nothing," I said.

She gave a long sigh.

"I'm so frightened," she said. "Charles, I'm so frightened . . ."

Her fear was very real. It communicated itself to me there in that narrow space. I wanted to reassure her, to help her. I had once more that poignant sense of her as terribly alone in hostile surroundings.

She might well have cried out: *Who is on my side?*

And what would the answer have been? Laurence Brown? And what, after all, was Laurence Brown? No tower of strength in a time of trouble. One of the weaker vessels. I remembered the two of them drifting in from the garden the night before.

I wanted to help her. I badly wanted to help her. But there was nothing much I could say or do. And I had at the bottom of my mind an embarrassed guilty feeling, as though Sophia's scornful eyes were watching me. I remembered Sophia's voice saying: "So she got you."

And Sophia did not see, did not want to see, Brenda's side of it. Alone, suspected of murder, with no one to stand by her.

"The inquest is to-morrow," Brenda said. "What—what will happen?"

There I could reassure her.

"Nothing," I said. "You needn't worry about that. It will be adjourned for the police to make inquiries. It will probably set the Press loose, though. So far, there's been no indication in the papers that it wasn't a natural death. The Leonides have got a good deal of influence. But with an adjourned inquest—well, the fun will start."

(What extraordinary things one said! The *fun*! Why must I choose that particular word?)

"Will—will they be very dreadful?"

110

"I shouldn't give any interviews if I were you. You know, Brenda, you ought to have a lawyer——" She recoiled with a terrific gasp of dismay. "No—no—not the way you mean. But someone to look after your interests and advise you as to procedure, and what to say and do, and what not to say and do.

"You see," I added, "you're very much alone."

Her hand pressed my arm more closely.

"Yes," she said. "You do understand that. You've helped, Charles, you have helped . . ."

I went down the stairs with a feeling of warmth, of satisfaction . . . Then I saw Sophia standing by the front door. Her voice was cold and rather dry.

"What a long time you've been," she said. "They rang up for you from London. Your father wants you."

"At the Yard?"

"Yes."

"I wonder what they want me for. They didn't say?"

Sophia shook her head. Her eyes were anxious. I drew her to me.

"Don't worry, darling," I said, "I'll soon be back."

XVII

THERE WAS something strained in the atmosphere of my father's room. The Old Man sat behind his table, Chief-Inspector Taverner leaned against the window frame. In the visitors' chair sat Mr. Gaitskill, looking ruffled.

"—extraordinary want of confidence," he was saying acidly.

"Of course, of course." My father spoke soothingly. "Ah, hallo, Charles, you've made good time. Rather a surprising development has occurred."

"Unprecedented," Mr. Gaitskill said.

Something had clearly ruffled the little lawyer to the core. Behind him, Chief-Inspector Taverner grinned at me.

"If I may recapitulate?" my father said. "Mr. Gaitskill received a somewhat surprising communication this morning, Charles. It was from a Mr. Agrodopolous, proprietor of the Delphos Restaurant. He is a very old man, a Greek by birth, and when he was a young man he was helped and befriended by Aristide Leonides. He has always remained deeply grateful to his friend and benefactor and it seems that

Aristide Leonides placed great reliance and trust in him."

"I would never have believed Leonides was of such a suspicious and secretive nature," said Mr. Gaitskill. "Of course, he was of advanced years—practically in his dotage one might say."

"Nationality tells," said my father gently. "You see, Gaitskill, when you are very old your mind dwells a good deal on the days of your youth and the friends of your youth."

"But Leonides' affairs had been in my hands for well over forty years," said Mr. Gaitskill. "Forty-three years and six months to be precise."

Taverner grinned again.

"What happened?" I asked.

Mr. Gaitskill opened his mouth, but my father forestalled him.

"Mr. Agrodopolous stated in his communication that he was obeying certain instructions given him by his friend Aristide Leonides. Briefly, about a year ago he had been entrusted by Mr. Leonides with a sealed envelope which Mr Agrodopolous was to forward to Mr. Gaitskill immediately after Mr. Leonides' death. In the event of Mr. Agrodopolous dying first, his son, a godson of Mr. Leonides, was to carry out the same instructions. Mr. Agrodopolous apologises for the delay, but explains that he has been ill with pneumonia and only learned of his old friend's death yesterday afternoon."

"The whole business is most unprofessional," said Mr. Gaitskill.

"When Mr. Gaitskill had opened the sealed envelope and made himself acquainted with its contents, he decided that it was his duty——"

"Under the circumstances," said Mr. Gaitskill.

"To let us see the enclosures. They consist of a will, duly signed and attested, and a covering letter."

"So the will has turned up at last?" I said.

Mr. Gaitskill turned a bright purple.

"It is not the same will," he barked. "This is not the document I drew up at Mr. Leonides' request. This has been written out in his own hand, a most dangerous thing for any layman to do. It seems to have been Mr. Leonides' intention to make me look a complete fool."

Chief-Inspector Taverner endeavoured to inject a little balm into the prevailing bitterness.

"He was a very old gentleman, Mr. Gaitskill," he said. "They're inclined to be cranky when they get old, you know —not barmy, of course, but just a little eccentric."

Mr. Gaitskill sniffed.

"Mr. Gaitskill rang us up," my father said, "and appraised us of the main contents of the will and I asked him to come round and bring the two documents with him. I also rang you up, Charles."

I did not quite see why I had been rung up. It seemed to me singularly unorthodox procedure on both my father's and Taverner's part. I should have learnt about the will in due course, and it was really not my business at all how old Leonides had left his money.

"Is it a different will?" I asked. "I mean, does it dispose of his estate in a different way?"

"It does indeed," said Mr. Gaitskill.

My father was looking at me. Chief-Inspector Taverner was very carefully not looking at me. In some way, I felt vaguely uneasy . . .

Something was going on in both their minds—and it was a something to which I had no clue.

I looked inquiringly at Gaitskill.

"It's none of my business," I said. "But——"

He responded.

"Mr. Leonides' testamentary dispositions are not, of course, a secret," he said. "I conceived it to be my duty to lay the facts before the police authorities first, and to be guided by them in my subsequent procedure. I understand," he paused, "that there is an—understanding, shall we say—between you and Miss Sophia Leonides?"

"I hope to marry her," I said, "but she will not consent to an engagement at the present time."

"Very proper," said Mr. Gaitskill.

I disagreed with him. But this was no time for argument.

"By this will," said Mr. Gaitskill, "dated November the 29th of last year, Mr. Leonides, after a bequest to his wife of one hundred thousand pounds, leaves his entire estate, real and personal, to his granddaughter, Sophia Katherine Leonides absolutely."

I gasped. Whatever I had expected, it was not this.

113

"He left the whole caboodle to Sophia," I said. "What an extraordinary thing. Any reason?"

"He set out his reasons very clearly in the covering letter," said my father. He picked up a sheet of paper from the desk in front of him. "You have no objection to Charles reading this, Mr. Gaitskill?"

"I am in your hands," said Mr. Gaitskill coldly. "The letter does at least offer an explanation—and possibly (though I am doubtful as to this) an excuse for Mr. Leonides' extraordinary conduct."

The Old Man handed me the letter. It was written in a small crabbed handwriting in very black ink. The handwriting showed character and individuality. It was not at all like the careful forming of the letters, more characteristic of a bygone period, when literacy was something painstakingly acquired and correspondingly valued.

Dear Gaitskill [it ran],

You will be astonished to get this, and probably offended. But I have my own reasons for behaving in what may seem to you an unnecessarily secretive manner. I have long been a believer in the individual. In a family (this I have observed in my boyhood and never forgotten) there is always one strong character and it usually falls to this one person to care for, and bear the burden of, the rest of the family. In my family I was that person. I came to London, established myself there, supported my mother and my aged grandparents in Smyrna, extricated one of my brothers from the grip of the law, secured the freedom of my sister from an unhappy marriage and so on. God has been pleased to grant me a long life, and I have been able to watch over and care for my own children and their children. Many have been taken from me by death; the rest, I am happy to say, are under my roof. When I die, the burden I have carried must descend on some-one else. I have debated whether to divide my fortune as equally as possible amongst my dear ones—but to do so would not eventually result in a proper equality. Men are not born equal—to offset the natural inequality of Nature one must redress the balance. In other words, someone must be my successor, must take upon him or herself the burden of responsibility for the rest of the family. After close observation I do not consider either of my sons fit

114

or this responsibility. My dearly loved son Roger has no business sense, and though of a lovable nature is too impulsive to have good judgment. My son Philip is too unsure of himself to do anything but retreat from life. Eustace, my grandson, is very young and I do not think he has the qualities of sense and judgment necessary. He is indolent and very easily influenced by the ideas of anyone whom he meets. Only my granddaughter Sophia seems to me to have the positive qualities required. She has brains, judgment, courage, a fair and unbiased mind and, I think, generosity of spirit. To her I commit the family welfare—and the welfare of my kind sister-in-law Edith de Haviland, for whose life-long devotion to the family I am deeply grateful.

This explains the enclosed document. What will be harder to explain—or rather to explain to you, my old friend—is the deception that I have employed. I thought it wise not to raise speculation about the disposal of my money, and I have no intention of letting my family know that Sophia is to be my heir. Since my two sons have already had considerable fortunes settled upon them, I do not feel that my testamentary dispositions will place them in a humiliating position.

To stifle curiosity and surmise, I asked you to draw me up a will. This will I read aloud to my assembled family. I laid it on my desk, placed a sheet of blotting paper over it and asked for two servants to be summoned. When they came I slid the blotting paper up a little, exposing the bottom of a document, signed my name and caused them to signs theirs. I need hardly say that what I and they signed was the will which I now enclose and *not* the one drafted by you which I had read aloud.

I cannot hope that you will understand what prompted me to execute this trick. I will merely ask you to forgive me for keeping you in the dark. A very old man likes to keep his little secrets.

Thank you, my dear friend, for the assiduity with which you have always attended to my affairs. Give Sophia my dear love. Ask her to watch over the family well and shield them from harm.

Yours very sincerely,
Aristide Leonides.

I read this very remarkable document with intense interes[t]

"Extraordinary," I said.

"Most extraordinary," said Mr. Gaitskill, rising. "I repeat, think my old friend Mr. Leonides might have trusted *me*."

"No, Gaitskill," said my father. "He was a natural twiste[r] He liked, if I may put it so, doing things the crooked way."

"That's right, sir," said Chief-Inspector Taverner. "He wa[s] a twister if there ever was one!"

He spoke with feeling.

Gaitskill stalked out unmollified. He had been wounded t[o] the depths of his professional nature.

"It's hit him hard," said Taverner. "Very respectable firm Gaitskill, Callum & Gaitskill. No hanky panky with them When old Leonides put through a doubtful deal, he neve[r] put it through with Gaitskill, Callum & Gaitskill. He ha[d] half a dozen different firms of solicitors who acted for him Oh, he was a twister!"

"And never more so than when making his will," sai[d] my father.

"We were fools," said Taverner. "When you come to thin[k] of it, the only person who *could* have played tricks with tha[t] will was the old boy himself. It just never occurred to u[s] that he could want to!"

I remembered Josephine's superior smile as she had said: "Aren't the police *stupid*?"

But Josephine had not been present on the occasion o[f] the will. And even if she had been listening outside th[e] door (which I was fully prepared to believe!) she coul[d] hardly have guessed what her grandfather was doing. Why then, the superior air? What did she know that made her say the police were stupid? Or was it, again, just showing off?

Struck by the silence in the room I looked up sharpl[y] —both my father and Taverner were watching me. I don'[t] know what there was in their manner that compelled me t[o] blurt out defiantly:

"Sophia knew nothing about this! Nothing at all."

"No?" said my father.

I didn't quite know whether it was an agreement or [a] question.

"She'll be absolutely astounded!"

"Yes?"

"Astounded!"

116

There was a pause. Then, with what seemed sudden harshness, the telephone on my father's desk rang.

"Yes?" He lifted the receiver—listened and then said: "put her through."

He looked at me.

"It's your young woman," he said. "She wants to speak to us. It's urgent."

I took the receiver from him.

"Sophia?"

"Charles? Is that you? It's—Josephine!" Her voice broke slightly.

"What about Josephine?"

"She's been hit on the head. Concussion. She's—she's pretty bad . . . They say she may not recover . . ."

I turned to the other two.

"Josephine's been knocked out," I said.

My father took the receiver from me. He said sharply as he did so:

"I told you to keep an eye on that child . . ."

XVIII

In NEXT to no time Taverner and I were racing in a fast police car in the direction of Swinly Dean.

I remembered Josephine emerging, from among the cisterns, and her airy remark that it was "about time for the second murder." The poor child had had no idea that she herself was likely to be the victim of the "second murder."

I accepted fully the blame that my father had tacitly ascribed to me. Of course I ought to have kept an eye on Josephine. Though neither Taverner nor I had any real clue to the poisoner of old Leonides, it was highly possible that Josephine had. What I had taken for childish nonsense and "showing off" might very well have been something quite different. Josephine, in her favourite sports of snooping and prying, might have become aware of some piece of information that she herself could not assess at its proper value.

I remembered the twig that had cracked in the garden.

I had had an inkling then that danger was about. I had acted upon it at the moment, and afterwards it had seemed to me that my suspicions had been melodramatic and unreal.

On the contrary, I should have realised that this wa
murder, that whoever had committed murder had endangere
their neck, and that consequently that same person would no
hesitate to repeat the crime if by that way safety could b
assured.

Perhaps Magda, by some obscure maternal instinct, had
recognised that Josephine was in peril, and that may hav
been what occasioned her sudden feverish haste to get th
child sent to Switzerland.

Sophia came out to meet us as we arrived. Josephine, sh
said, had been taken by ambulance to Market Basing Genera
Hospital. Dr. Gray would let them know as soon as possibl
the result of the X-ray.

"How did it happen?" asked Taverner.

Sophia led the way round to the back of the house and
through a door in a small disused yard. In one corner a
door stood ajar.

"It's a kind of wash-house," Sophia explained. "There'
a cat hole cut in the bottom of the door, and Josephine used
to stand on it and swing to and fro."

I remembered swinging on doors in my own youth.

The wash-house was small and rather dark. There were
wooden boxes in it, some old hose pipe, a few derelict
garden implements, and some broken furniture. Just inside the
door was a marble lion door-stop.

"It's the door-stopper from the front door," Sophia explained. "It must have been balanced on top of the door."

Taverner reached up a hand to the top of the door. It was
a low door, the top of it only about a foot above his head.

"A booby trap," he said.

He swung the door experimentally to and fro. Then he
stooped to the block of marble but he did not touch it.

"Has anyone handled this?"

"No," said Sophia. "I wouldn't let anyone touch it."

"Quite right. Who found her?"

"I did. She didn't come in for her dinner at one o'clock.
Nannie was calling her. She'd passed through the kitchen and
out into the stable yard about a quarter of an hour before. Nannie said, 'She'll be bouncing her ball or swinging on
that door again.' I said I'd fetch her in."

Sophia paused.

118

"She had a habit of playing in that way, you said? Who knew about that?"

Sophia shrugged her shoulders.

"Pretty well everybody in the house, I should think."

"Who else used the wash-house? Gardeners?"

Sophia shook her head.

"Hardly anyone ever goes into it."

"And this little yard isn't overlooked from the house?" Taverner summed it up. "Anyone could have slipped out from the house or round the front and fixed up that trap ready. But it would be chancy ..."

He broke off, looking at the door, and swinging it gently to and fro.

"Nothing certain about it. Hit or miss. And likelier miss than hit. But she was unlucky. With her it was hit."

Sophia shivered.

He peered at the floor. There were various dents on it.

"Looks as though someone experimented first . . . to see just how it would fall . . . The sound wouldn't carry to the house."

"No, we didn't hear anything. We'd no idea anything was wrong until I came out and found her lying face down—all sprawled out." Sophia voice broke a little. "There was blood on her hair."

"That her scarf?" Taverner pointed to a checked woollen muffler lying on the floor.

"Yes."

Using the scarf he picked up the block of marble carefully.

"There may be fingerprints," he said, but he spoke without much hope. "But I rather think whoever did it was —careful." He said to me: "What are you looking at?"

I was looking at a broken-backed wooden kitchen chair which was among the derelicts. On the seat of it were a few fragments of earth.

"Curious," said Taverner. "Someone stood on that chair with muddy feet. Now why was that?"

He shook his head.

"What time was it when you found her, Miss Leonides?"

"It must have been five minutes past one."

"And your Nannie saw her going out about twenty minutes earlier. Who was the last person before that known to have been in the wash-house?"

"I've no idea. Probably Josephine herself. Josephine was swinging on the door this morning after breakfast, I know."

Taverner nodded.

"So between then and a quarter to one *someone set the trap*. You say that bit of marble is the door-stop you use for the front door? Any idea when that was missing?"

Sophia shook her head.

"The door hasn't been propped open all to-day. It's been too cold."

"Any idea where everyone was all the morning?"

"I went out for a walk. Eustace and Josephine did lessons until half-past twelve—with a break at half-past ten. Father, I think, has been in the library all the morning."

"Your mother?"

"She was just coming out of her bedroom when I came in from my walk—that was about a quarter past twelve. She doesn't get up very early."

We re-entered the house. I followed Sophia to the library. Philip, looking white and haggard, sat in his usual chair. Magda crouched against his knees, crying quietly. Sophia asked:

"Have they telephoned yet from the hospital?"

Philip shook his head.

Magda sobbed.

"Why wouldn't they let me go with her? My baby—my funny ugly baby. And I used to call her a changeling and make her so angry. How could I be so cruel? And now she'll die. I know she'll die."

"Hush, my dear," said Philip. "Hush."

I felt that I had no place in this family scene of anxiety and grief. I withdrew quietly and went to find Nannie. She was sitting in the kitchen crying quietly.

"It's a judgment on me, Mr. Charles, for the hard things I've been thinking. A judgment, that's what it is."

I did not try and fathom her meaning.

"There's wickedness in this house. That's what there is. I didn't wish to see it or believe it. But seeing's believing. Somebody killed the master and the same somebody must have tried to kill Josephine."

"Why should they try and kill Josephine?"

Nannie removed a corner of her handkerchief from her eye and gave me a shrewd glance.

"You know well enough what she was like, Mr. Charles. She liked to know things. She was always like that, even as a tiny thing. Used to hide under the dinner table and listen to the maids talking and then she'd hold it over them. Made her feel important. You see, she was passed over, as it were, by the mistress. She wasn't a handsome child, like the other two. She was always a plain little thing. A changeling, the mistress used to call her. I blame the mistress for that, for it's my belief it turned the child sour. But in a funny sort of way she got her own back by finding out things about people and letting them know she knew them. But it isn't safe to do that when there's a poisoner about!"

No, it hadn't been safe. And that brought something else to my mind. I asked Nannie: "Do you know where she kept a little black book—a note-book of some kind where she used to write down things?"

"I know what you mean, Mr. Charles. Very sly about it, she was. I've seen her sucking her pencil and writing in the book and sucking her pencil again. And 'don't do that,' I'd say, 'you'll get lead poisoning' and 'oh no, I shan't,' she said, 'because it isn't really lead in a pencil. It's carbon,' though I don't see how *that* could be so for if you call a thing a lead pencil it stands to reason that that's because there's lead in it."

"You'd think so," I agreed. "But as a matter of fact she was right." (Josephine was always right!) "What about this note-book? Do you know where she kept it?"

"I've no idea at all, sir. It was one of the things she was sly about."

"She hadn't got it with her when she was found?"

"Oh no, Mr. Charles, there was no note-book."

Had someone taken the note-book? Or had she hidden it in her own room? The idea came to me to look and see. I was not sure which Josephine's room was, but as I stood hesitating in the passage Taverner's voice called me:

"Come in here," he said. "I'm in the kid's room. Did you ever see such a sight?"

I stepped over the threshold and stopped dead.

The small room looked as though it had been visited by a tornado. The drawers of the chest of drawers were pulled out and their contents scattered on the floor. The mattress and bedding had been pulled from the small bed. The rugs were tossed into heaps. The chairs had been turned upside down, the pictures taken down from the wall, the photographs wrenched out of their frames.

"Good Lord," I exclaimed. "What was the big idea?"

"What do you think?"

"Someone was looking for something."

"Exactly."

I looked round and whistled.

"But who on earth—surely nobody could come in here and do all this and not be heard—or seen?"

"Why not? Mrs. Leonides spends the morning in her bedroom doing her nails and ringing up her friends on the telephone and playing with her clothes. Philip sits in the library browsing over books. The nurse woman is in the kitchen peeling potatoes and stringing beans. In a family that knows each other's habits it would be easy enough. And I'll tell you this. Anyone in the house could have done our little job —could have set the trap for the child and wrecked her room. But it was someone in a hurry, someone who hadn't the time to search quietly."

"Anyone in the house, you say?"

"Yes, I've checked up. Everyone has some time or other unaccounted for. Philip, Magda, the nurse, your girl. The same upstairs. Brenda spent most of the morning alone. Laurence and Eustace had a half hour break—from ten-thirty to eleven—you were with them part of that time—but not all of it. Miss de Haviland was in the garden alone. Roger was in his study."

"Only Clemency was in London at her job."

"No, even she isn't out of it. She stayed at home to-day with a headache—she was alone in her room having that headache. Any of them—any blinking one of them! And I don't know which! I've no idea. If I knew what they were looking for in here——"

His eyes went round the wrecked room . . .

"And if I knew whether they'd found it . . ."

Something stirred in my brain—a memory . . .,

Taverner clinched it by asking me:

"What was the kid doing when you last saw her?"

"Wait," I said.

I dashed out of the room and up the stairs. I passed through the left-hand door and went up to the top floor. I pushed open the door of the cistern room, mounted the two steps and bending my head, since the ceiling was low and sloping, I looked round me.

Josephine had said when I asked her what she was doing there that she was "detecting."

I didn't see what there could be to detect in a cobwebby attic full of water tanks. But such an attic would make a good hiding-place. I considered it probable that Josephine had been hiding something there, something that she knew quite well she had no business to have. If so, it oughtn't to take long to find it.

It took me just three minutes. Tucked away behind the largest tank, from the interior of which a sibilant hissing added an eerie note to the atmosphere, I found a packet of letters wrapped in a torn piece of brown paper.

I read the first letter.

Oh Laurence—my darling, my own dear love . . . It was wonderful last night when you quoted that verse of poetry. I knew it was meant for me, though you didn't look at me. Aristide said, "You read verse well." He didn't guess what we were both feeling. My darling, I feel convinced that soon everything will come right. We shall be glad that he never knew, that he died happy. He's been good to me. I don't want him to suffer. But I don't really think that it can be any pleasure to live after you're eighty. I shouldn't want to! Soon we shall be together for always. How wonderful it will be when I can say to you: "My dear dear husband . . ." Dearest, we were made for each other. I love you, love you, love you—I can see no end to our love, I——

There was a good deal more, but I had no wish to go on.

Grimly I went downstairs and thrust my parcel into Taverner's hands.

"It's possible," I said, "that that's what our unknown friend was looking for."

Taverner read a few passages, whistled and shuffled through the various letters.

Then he looked at me with the expression of a cat who has been fed with the best cream.

"Well," he said softly. "This pretty well cooks Mrs. Brenda Leonides' goose. *And* Mr. Laurence Brown's. So it *was* them, all the time . . ."

XIX

It SEEMS odd to me, looking back, how suddenly and completely my pity and sympathy for Brenda Leonides vanished with the discovery of her letters, the letters she had written to Laurence Brown. Was my vanity unable to stand up to the revelation that she loved Laurence Brown with a doting and sugary infatuation and had deliberately lied to me? I don't know. I'm not a psychologist. I prefer to believe that it was the thought of the child Josephine, struck down in ruthless self-preservation, that dried up the springs of my sympathy.

"Brown fixed that booby trap, if you ask me," said Taverner, "and it explains what puzzled me about it."

"What did puzzle you?"

"Well, it was such a sappy thing to do. Look here, say the kid's got hold of these letters—letters that are absolutely damning! The first thing to do is to try and get them back (after all, if the kid talks about them, but has got nothing to show, it can be put down as mere romancing), but you can't get them back because you can't find them. Then the only thing to do is to put the kid out of action for good. You've done one murder and you're not squeamish about doing another. You know she's fond of swinging on a door in a disused yard. The ideal thing to do is wait behind the door and lay her out as she comes through with a poker, or an iron bar, or a nice bit of hose-pipe. They're all there ready to hand. Why fiddle about with a marble lion perched on top of a door which is as likely as not to miss her altogether and which even if it *does* fall on her may not do the job properly (which actually is how it turns out). I ask you—*why*?"

"Well," I said, "what's the answer?"

"The only idea I got to begin with was that it was intended to tie in with someone's alibi. Somebody would have a nice fat alibi for the time when Josephine was being slugged. But that doesn't wash because, to begin with, nobody seems to have any kind of alibi, and second, someone's bound to look for the child at lunch time, and they'll find the booby trap and the marble block, the whole *modus operandi* will be quite plain to see. Of course, *if* the murderer had removed the block before the child was found, then we might have been puzzled. But as it is the whole thing just doesn't make sense."

He stretched out his hands.

"And what's your present explanation?"

"The personal element. Personal idiosyncrasy. Laurence Brown's idiosyncrasy. *He doesn't like violence—he can't force himself to do physical violence. He* literally *couldn't have stood behind the door and socked the kid on the head. He could* rig up a booby trap and go away and not see it happen."

"Yes, I see," I said slowly. "It's the eserine in the insulin bottle all over again?"

"Exactly."

"Do you think he did that without Brenda's knowing?"

"It would explain why she didn't throw away the insulin bottle. Of course, they may have fixed it up between them—or she may have thought up the poison trick all by herself—a nice easy death for her tired old husband and all for the best in the best possible worlds! But I bet she didn't fix the booby trap. Women never have any faith in mechanical things working properly. And they are right. I think myself the eserine was her idea, but that she made her besotted slave do the switch. She's the kind that usually manages to avoid doing anything equivocal themselves. Then they keep a nice happy conscience."

He paused, then went on:

"With these letters I think the D.P.P. will say we have a case. They'll take a bit of explaining away! Then, if the kid gets through all right everything in the garden will be lovely." He gave me a sideways glance. "How does it feel to be engaged to about a million pounds sterling?"

I winced. In the excitement of the last few hours, I had forgotten the developments about the will.

"Sophia doesn't know yet," I said. "Do you want me to tell her?"

"I understand Gaitskill is going to break the sad (or glad) news after the inquest to-morrow." Taverner paused and looked at me thoughtfully.

"I wonder," he said, "what the reactions will be from the family?"

XX

THE INQUEST went off much as I had prophesied. It was adjourned at the request of the police.

We were in good spirits, for news had come through the night before from the hospital that Josephine's injuries were much less serious than had been feared and that her recovery would be rapid. For the moment, Dr. Gray said, she was to be allowed no visitors—not even her mother.

"Particularly not her mother," Sophia murmured to me. "I made that quite clear to Dr. Gray. Anyway, he knows mother."

I must have looked rather doubtful, for Sophia said sharply:

"Why the disapproving look?"

"Well—surely a mother——"

"I'm glad you've got a few nice old-fashioned ideas, Charles. But you don't quite know what my mother is capable of yet. The darling can't help it, but there would simply have to be a grand dramatic scene. And dramatic scenes aren't the best things for anyone recovering from head injuries."

"You do think of everything, don't you, my sweet."

"Well, somebody's got to do the thinking now that grandfather's gone."

I looked at her speculatively. I saw that old Leonides' acumen had not deserted him. The mantle of his responsibilities was already on Sophia's shoulders.

After the inquest, Gaitskill accompanied us back to Three Gables. He cleared his throat and said pontifically:

"There is an announcement it is my duty to make to you all."

For this purpose the family assembled in Magda's drawing-room. I had on this occasion the rather pleasurable sensations of the man behind the scenes. I knew in advance what Gaitskill had to say.

I prepared myself to observe the reactions of everyone.

Gaitskill was brief and dry. Any signs of personal feeling and annoyance were well held in check. He read first Aristide Leonides' letter and then the will itself.

It was very interesting to watch. I only wished my eyes could be everywhere at once.

I did not pay much attention to Brenda and Laurence. The provision for Brenda in this will was the same. I watched primarily Roger and Philip, and after them Magda and Clemency.

My first impression was that they all behaved very well.

Philip's lips were pressed closely together, his handsome head was thrown back against the tall chair in which he was sitting. He did not speak.

Magda, on the contrary, burst into speech as soon as Mr. Gaitskill finished, her rich voice surging over his thin tones like an incoming tide drowning a rivulet.

"Darling Sophia—how extraordinary—how *romantic*. Fancy old Sweetie Pie being so cunning and deceitful—just like a dear old baby. Didn't he trust us? Did he think we'd be cross? He never seemed to be fonder of Sophia than the rest of us. But really, it's most dramatic."

Suddenly Magda jumped lightly to her feet, danced over to Sophia and swept her a very grand court curtsey.

"Madame Sophia, your penniless and broken-down-old mother begs you for alms." Her voice took on a Cockney whine. "Spare us a copper, old dear. Your Ma wants to go to the pictures."

Her hand, crooked into a claw, twitched urgently at Sophia.

Philip, without moving, said through stiff lips:

"Please, Magda, there's no call for any unnecessary clowning."

"Oh, but Roger," cried Magda, suddenly turning to Roger. "Poor darling Roger. Sweetie was going to come to the rescue and then, before he could do it, he died. And now Roger doesn't get *anything*. Sophia," she turned imperiously, "you simply must do something about Roger."

"No," said Clemency. She had moved forward a step. Her face was defiant. "Nothing. Nothing at all."

Roger came shambling over to Sophia like a large amiable bear.

He took her hands affectionately.

"I don't want a penny, my dear girl. As soon as this business is cleared up—or has died down, which is more what it looks like—then Clemency and I are off to the West Indies and the simple life. If I'm ever in extremis I'll apply to the head of the family"—he grinned at her engagingly —"but until then I don't want a penny. I'm a very simple

127

person really, my dear—you ask Clemency if I'm not."

An unexpected voice broke in. It was Edith de Haviland's.

"That's all very well," she said. "But you've got to pay some attention to the look of the thing. If you go bankrupt, Roger, and then slink off to the ends of the earth without Sophia's holding out a helping hand, there will be a good deal of ill-natured talk that will not be pleasant for Sophia."

"What does public opinion matter?" asked Clemency scornfully.

"We know it doesn't to you, Clemency," said Edith de Haviland sharply, "but Sophia lives in *this* world. She's a girl with good brains and a good heart, and I've no doubt that Aristide was quite right in his selection of her to hold the family fortunes—though to pass over your two sons in their lifetime seems odd to our English ideas—but I think it would be very unfortunate if it got about that she behaved greedily over this—and had let Roger crash without trying to help him."

Roger went over to his aunt. He put his arms round her and hugged her.

"Aunt Edith," he said. "You are a darling—and a stubborn fighter, but you don't begin to understand. Clemency and I know what we want—and what we don't want!"

Clemency, a sudden spot of colour showing in each thin cheek, stood defiantly facing them.

"None of you," she said, "understand Roger. You never have! I don't suppose you ever will! Come on, Roger."

They left the room as Mr. Gaitskill began clearing his throat and arranging his papers. His countenance was one of deep disapprobation. He had disliked the foregoing scenes very much. That was clear.

My eyes came at last to Sophia herself. She stood straight and handsome by the fireplace, her chin up, her eyes steady. She had just been left an immense fortune, but my principal thought was how alone she had suddenly become. Between her and her family a barrier had been erected. Henceforth she was divided from them, and I fancied that she already knew and faced that fact. Old Leonides had laid a burden upon her shoulders—he had been aware of that and she knew it herself. He had believed that her shoulders were strong enough to bear it, but just at this moment I felt unutterably sorry for her.

So far she had not spoken—indeed she had been given

no chance, but very soon now speech would be forced from her. Already, beneath the affection of her family, I could sense latent hostility. Even in Magda's graceful play-acting there had been, I fancied, a subtle malice. And there were other darker undercurrents that had not yet come to the surface.

Mr. Gaitskill's throat clearings gave way to precise and measured speech.

"Allow me to congratulate you, Sophia," he said. "You are a very wealthy woman. I should not advise any—er —precipitate action. I can advance you what ready money is needed for current expenses. If you wish to discuss future arrangements I shall be happy to give you the best advice in my power. Make an appointment with me at Lincoln's Inn when you have had plenty of time to think things over."

"Roger," began Edith de Haviland obstinately.

Mr. Gaitskill snapped in quickly.

"Roger," he said, "must fend for himself. He's a grown man—er, fifty-four, I believe. And Aristide Leonides was quite right, you know. He isn't a business man. Never will be." He looked at Sophia. "If you put Associated Catering on its legs again, don't be under any illusions that Roger can run it successfully."

"I shouldn't dream of putting Associated Catering on its legs again," said Sophia.

It was the first time she had spoken. Her voice was crisp and businesslike.

"It would be an idiotic thing to do," she added.

Gaitskill shot a glance at her from under his brows, and smiled to himself. Then he wished everyone good-bye and went out.

There were a few moments of silence, a realisation that the family circle was alone with itself.

Then Philip got up stiffly.

"I must get back to the library," he said. "I have lost a lot of time."

"Father——" Sophia spoke uncertainly, almost pleadingly.

I felt her quiver and draw back as Philip turned cold hostile eyes on her.

"You must forgive me not congratulating you," he said. "But this has been rather a shock to me. I would not have believed that my father would have so humiliated me—that he would have disregarded my lifetime's devotion—yes—devotion."

For the first time, the natural man broke through th crust of icy restraint.

"My God," he cried. "How could he do this to me? H was always unfair to me—always."

"Oh no, Philip, no, you mustn't think that," cried Edith de Haviland. "Don't regard this as another slight. It isn' When people get old, they turn naturally to a younge generation . . . I assure you it's only that . . . and beside Aristide had a very keen business sense. I've often heard hir say that two lots of death duties——"

"He never cared for me," said Philip. His voice was lo and hoarse. "It was always Roger—Roger. Well, at least —an extraordinary expression of spite suddenly marred hi handsome features—"father realised that Roger was a foo and a failure. He cut Roger out, too."

"What about me?" said Eustace.

I had hardly noticed Eustace until now, but I perceive that he was trembling with some violent emotion. His fac was crimson, there were, I thought, tears in his eyes. His voic shook as it rose hysterically.

"It's a shame!" said Eustace. "It's a damned shame! Hov dare grandfather do this to me? How dare he? I was hi only grandson. How dare he pass me over for Sophia? It' not fair. I hate him. I hate him. I'll never forgive him a long as I live. Beastly tyrannical old man. I wanted him to die. I wanted to get out of this house. I wanted to b my own master. And now I've got to be bullied and messe around by Sophia, and be made to look a fool. I wish was dead . . ."

His voice broke and he rushed out of the room.

Edith de Haviland gave a sharp click of her tongue.

"No self-control," she murmured.

"I know just how he feels," cried Magda.

"I'm sure you do," said Edith with acidity in her tone.

"The poor sweet! I must go after him."

"Now, Magda——" Edith hurried after her.

Their voices died away. Sophia remained looking at Philip There was, I think, a certain pleading in her glance. If so, i got no response. He looked at her coldly, quite in control o himself once more.

130

"You played your cards very well, Sophia," he said and went out of the room.

"That was a cruel thing to say," I cried. "Sophia——"

She stretched out her hands to me. I took her in my arms.

"This is too much for you, my sweet."

"I know just how they feel," said Sophia.

"That old devil, your grandfather, shouldn't have let you in for this."

She straightened her shoulders.

"He believed I could take it. And so I can. I wish—I wish Eustace didn't mind so much."

"He'll get over it."

"Will he? I wonder. He's the kind that broods terribly. And I hate father being hurt."

"Your mother's all right."

"She minds a bit. It goes against the grain to have to come and ask your daughter for money to put on plays. She'll be after me to put on the Edith Thompson one before you can turn round."

"And what will you say? If it keeps her happy . . ."

Sophia pulled herself right out of my arms, her head went back.

"I shall say *No*! It's a rotten play and mother couldn't play the part. It would be throwing the money away."

I laughed softly. I couldn't help it.

"What is it?" Sophia demanded suspiciously.

"I'm beginning to understand why your grandfather left you his money. You're a chip off the old block, Sophia."

XXI

MY ONE feeling of regret at this time was that Josephine was out of it all. She would have enjoyed it all so much.

Her recovery was rapid and she was expected to be back any day now, but nevertheless she missed another event of importance.

I was in the rock garden one morning with Sophia and Brenda when a car drew up to the front door. Taverner and Sergeant Lamb got out of it. They went up the steps and into the house.

Brenda stood still, staring at the car.

"It's those men," she said. "They've come back, and I thought they'd given up—I thought it was all over."

I saw her shiver.

She had joined us about ten minutes before. Wrapped in her chinchilla coat, she had said: "If I don't get some air and exercise, I shall go mad. If I go outside the gate there's always a reporter waiting to pounce on me. It's like being besieged. Will it go on for ever?"

Sophia said that she supposed the reporters would soon get tired of it.

"You can go out in the car," she added.

"I tell you I want to get some exercise."

Then she said abruptly:

"You're giving Laurence the sack, Sophia. Why?"

Sophia answered quietly:

"We're making other arrangements for Eustace. And Josephine is going to Switzerland."

"Well, you've upset Laurence very much. He feels you don't trust him."

Sophia did not reply and it was at that moment that Taverner's car had arrived.

Standing there, shivering in the moist autumn air, Brenda muttered: "What do they want? Why have they come?"

I thought I knew why they had come. I said nothing to Sophia of the letters I had found by the cistern, but I knew that they had gone to the Director of Public Prosecutions.

Taverner came out of the house again. He walked across the drive and the lawn towards us. Brenda shivered more violently.

"What does he want?" she repeated nervously. "What does he want?"

Then Taverner was with us. He spoke curtly in his official voice, using the official phrases.

"I have a warrant here for your arrest—you are charged with administering eserine to Aristide Leonides on September 19th last. I must warn you that anything you say may be used in evidence at your trial."

And then Brenda went to pieces. She screamed. She clung to me. She cried out, "No, no, no, it isn't true! Charles, tell them it isn't true! I didn't do it. I didn't know anything about it. It's all a plot. Don't let them take me away. It isn't

ue, I tell you . . . It *isn't true* . . . I haven't done any-
ing . . ."

It was horrible—unbelievably horrible. I tried to soothe
er, I unfastened her fingers from my arm. I told her that
would arrange for a lawyer for her—that she was to keep
alm—that a lawyer would arrange everything——

Taverner took her gently under the elbow.

"Come along, Mrs. Leonides," he said. "You don't want
hat, do you? No? Then we'll go off right away."

She pulled back, staring at him with enormous cat's eyes.

"Laurence," she said. "What have you done to Laurence?"

"Mr. Laurence Brown is also under arrest," said Taverner.

She wilted then. Her body seemed to collapse and shrink.
he tears poured down her face. She went away quietly with
averner across the lawn to the car. I saw Laurence
rown and Sergeant Lamb come out of the house. They all got
to the car. The car drove away.

I drew a deep breath and turned to Sophia. She was very
ale and there was a look of distress on her face.

"It's horrible, Charles," she said. "It's quite horrible."

"I know."

"You must get her a really first-class solicitor—the best
here is. She—she must have all the help possible."

"One doesn't realise," I said, "what these things are like.
've never seen anyone arrested before."

"I know. One has no idea."

We were both silent. I was thinking of the desperate terror
n Brenda's face. It had seemed familiar to me and sud-
enly I realised why. It was the same expression that I had
een on Magda Leonides' face the first day I had come to the
Crooked House when she had been talking about the Edith
Thompson play.

"*And then,*" she had said, "*sheer terror*, don't you think
o?"

Sheer terror—that was what had been on Brenda's face.
Brenda was not a fighter. I wondered that she had ever
ad the nerve to do murder. But possibly she had not.
Possibly it had been Laurence Brown, with his persecution
mania, his unstable personality, who had put the contents of
ne little bottle into another little bottle—a simple easy
act—to free the woman he loved.

"So it's over," said Sophia.

She sighed deeply, then asked:

"But why arrest them now? I thought there wasn't enough evidence."

"A certain amount of evidence has come to light. Letters."

"You mean love letters between them?"

"Yes."

"What fools people are to keep these things!"

Yes, indeed. Fools. The kind of folly which never seemed to profit by the experience of others. You couldn't open a daily newspaper without coming across some instance of that folly—the passion to keep the written word, the written assurance of love.

"It's quite beastly, Sophia," I said. "But it's no good minding about it. After all, it's what we've been hoping all along, isn't it? It's what you said that first night at Mario's. You said it would be all right if the right person had killed your grandfather. Brenda was the right person, wasn't she? Brenda or Laurence?"

"Don't, Charles, you make me feel awful."

"But we must be sensible. We can marry now, Sophia. You can't hold me off any longer. The Leonides family are out of it."

She stared at me. I had never realised before the vivid blue of her eyes.

"Yes," she said. "I suppose we're out of it now. We *are* out of it, aren't we. You're sure?"

"My dear girl, none of you ever really had a shadow of motive."

Her face went suddenly white.

"Except me, Charles. *I* had a motive."

"Yes, of course——" I was taken aback. "But not really. You didn't know, you see, about the will."

"But I did, Charles," she whispered.

"What?" I stared at her. I felt suddenly cold.

"I knew all the time that grandfather had left his money to me."

"But how?"

"He told me. About a fortnight before he was killed. He said to me quite suddenly: 'I've left all my money to you, Sophia. You must look after the family when I've gone.' "

I stared.

"You never told me."

"No. You see, when they all explained about the will and

134

his signing it, I thought perhaps he had made a mistake—that he was just imagining that he had left it to me. Or that if he had made a will leaving it to me, then it had got lost and would never turn up. I didn't want it to turn up—I was afraid."

"Afraid? Why?"

"I suppose—because of murder."

I remembered the look of terror on Brenda's face—the wild unreasoning panic. I remembered the sheer panic that Magda had conjured up at will when she considered playing the part of a murderess. There would be no panic in Sophia's mind, but she was a realist, and she could see clearly enough that Leonides' will made her a suspect. I understood better now (or thought I did) her refusal to become engaged to me and her insistence that I should find out the truth. Nothing but the truth, she had said, was any good to her. I remembered the passion, the earnestness with which she had said it.

We had turned to walk towards the house and suddenly, at a certain spot, I remembered something else she had said.

She had said that she supposed she could murder someone, but if so, she had added, it must be for something really worth while.

XXII

ROUND A turn of the rock garden Roger and Clemency came walking briskly towards us. Roger's flapping tweeds suited him better than his City clothes. He looked eager and excited. Clemency was frowning.

"Hallo, you two," said Roger. "At last! I thought they were never going to arrest that foul woman. What they've been waiting for, I don't know. Well, they've pinched her now, and her miserable boy friend—and I hope they hang them both."

Clemency's frown increased. She said:

"Don't be so uncivilised, Roger."

"Uncivilised? Bosh! Deliberate cold-blooded poisoning of a helpless trusting old man—and when I'm glad the murderers are caught and will pay the penalty you say I'm uncivilised! I tell you I'd willingly strangle that woman myself."

He added:

"She was with you, wasn't she, when the police came fo
her? How did she take it?"

"It was horrible," said Sophia in a low voice. "She wa
scared out of her wits."

"Serve her right."

"Don't be vindictive," said Clemency.

"Oh, I know, dearest, but you can't understand. It wasn
your father. I *loved* my father. Don't you understand?
loved him!"

"I should understand by now," said Clemency.

Roger said to her, half-jokingly:

"You've no imagination, Clemency. Suppose it had bee
I who had been poisoned——?"

I saw the quick droop of her lids, her half-clenched hands
She said sharply: "Don't say things like that even in fun."

"Never mind, darling, we'll soon be away from all this."

We moved towards the house. Roger and Sophia walke
ahead and Clemency and I brought up the rear. She said:

"I suppose now—they'll let us go?"

"Are you so anxious to get off?" I asked.

"It's wearing me out."

I looked at her in surprise. She met my glance with
faint desperate smile and a nod of the head.

"Haven't you seen, Charles, that I'm fighting all th
time? Fighting for my happiness. For Roger's. I've been s
afraid the family would persuade him to stop in England
That we'd go on tangled up in the midst of them, stifle
with family ties. I was afraid Sophia would offer him a
income and that he'd stay in England because it would mea
greater comfort and amenities for me. The trouble wit
Roger is that he will *not* listen. He gets ideas in his hea
—and they're never the right ideas. He doesn't know
anything. And he's enough of a Leonides to think tha
happiness for a woman is bound up with comfort and money
But I will fight for my happiness—I will. I will get Roge
away and give him the life that suits him where he won'
feel a failure. I want him to myself—away from them al
—right away——"

She had spoken in a low hurried voice with a kind of
desperation that startled me. I had not realised how much o
edge she was. I had not realised, either, quite how desperat
and posessive was her feeling for Roger.

It brought back to my mind that odd quotation of Edith e Haviland's. She had quoted the line "this side idolatry" ith a peculiar intonation. I wondered if she had been inking of Clemency.

Roger, I thought, had loved his father better than he vould ever love anyone else, better even than his wife, evoted though he was to her. I realised for the first time how rgent was Clemency's desire to get her husband to herself. ove for Roger, I saw, made up her entire existence. He was er child, as well as her husband and her lover.

A car drove up to the front door.

"Hallo," I said. "Here's Josephine back."

Josephine and Magda got out of the car. Josephine had a andage round her head but otherwise looked remarkably well. She said at once:

"I want to see my goldfish," and started towards us and he pond.

"Darling," cried Magda, "you'd better come in first and ie down a little, and perhaps have a little nourishing soup."

"Don't fuss, Mother," said Josephine. "I'm quite all right, nd I hate nourishing soup."

Magda looked irresolute. I knew that Josephine had really een fit to depart from the hospital for some days, and that t was only a hint from Taverner that had kept here there. Ie was taking no chances on Josephine's safety until his uspects were safe under lock and key.

I said to Magda:

"I dare say fresh air will do her good. I'll go and keep an ye on her."

I caught Josephine up before she got to the pond.

"All sorts of things have been happening while you've been way," I said.

Josephine did not reply. She peered with her short-sighted eyes into the pond.

"I don't see Ferdinand," she said.

"Which is Ferdinand?"

"The one with four tails."

"That kind is rather amusing. I like that bright gold one."

"It's quite a common one."

"I don't much care for that moth-eaten white one."

Josephine cast me a scornful glance.

"That's a shebunkin. They cost a lot—far more than goldfish."

"Don't you want to hear what's been happening, Josephine?"

"I expect I know about it."

"Did you know that another will has been found and that your grandfather left all his money to Sophia?"

Josephine nodded in a bored kind of way.

"Mother told me. Anyway, I knew it already."

"Do you mean you heard it in hospital?"

"No, I mean I knew that grandfather had left his money to Sophia. I heard him tell her so."

"Were you listening again?"

"Yes. I like listening."

"It's a disgraceful thing to do, and remember this, listeners hear no good of themselves."

Josephine gave me a peculiar glance.

"I heard what he said about me to her, if that's what you mean."

She added:

"Nannie gets wild if she catches me listening at doors. She says it's not the sort of thing a little lady does."

"She's quite right."

"Pooh," said Josephine. "Nobody's a lady nowadays. They said so on the Brains Trust. They said it was ob-so-lete." She pronounced the word carefully.

I changed the subject.

"You've got home a bit late for the big event," I said. "Chief-Inspector Taverner has arrested Brenda and Laurence."

I expected that Josephine, in her character of young detective, would be thrilled by this information, but she merely repeated in her maddening bored fashion:

"Yes, I know."

"You can't know. It's only just happened."

"The car passed us on the road. Inspector Taverner and the detective with the suède shoes were inside with Brenda and Laurence, so of course I knew they must have been arrested. I hope he gave them the proper caution. You have to, you know."

I assured her that Taverner had acted strictly according to etiquette.

"I had to tell him about the letters," I said apologetically. "
138

ound them behind the cistern. I'd have let you tell him only you were knocked out."

Josephine's hand went gingerly to her head.

"I ought to have been killed," she said with complacency. 'I told you it was about time for the second murder. The cistern was a rotten place to hide those letters. I guessed at once when I saw Laurence coming out of there one day. I mean he's not a useful kind of man who does things with ball taps, or pipes or fuses, so I knew he must have been hiding something."

"But I thought——" I broke off as Edith de Haviland's voice called authoritatively:

"Josephine, Josephine, come here at once."

Josephine sighed.

"More fuss," she said. "But I'd better go. You have to, if it's Aunt Edith."

She ran across the lawn. I followed more slowly.

After a brief interchange of words Josephine went into the house. I joined Edith de Haviland on the terrace.

This morning she looked fully her age. I was startled by the lines of weariness and suffering on her face. She looked exhausted and defeated. She saw the concern in my face and tried to smile.

"That child seems none the worse for her adventure," she said. "We must look after her better in future. Still—I suppose now it won't be necessary?"

She sighed and said:

"I'm glad it's over. But what an exhibition! If you *are* arrested for murder, you might at least have some dignity. I've no patience with people like Brenda who go to pieces and squeal. No guts, these people. Laurence Brown looked like a cornered rabbit."

An obscure instinct of pity rose in me.

"Poor devils," I said.

"Yes—poor devils. She'll have the sense to look after herself, I suppose? I mean the right lawyers—all that sort of thing."

It was queer, I thought, the dislike they all had for Brenda, and their scrupulous care for her to have all the advantages for defence.

Edith de Haviland went on:

139

"How long will it be? How long will the whole thing take?"

I said I didn't know exactly. They would be charged at the police court and presumably sent for trial. Three or four months, I estimated—and if convicted, there would be the appeal.

"Do you think they will be convicted?" she asked.

"I don't know. I don't know exactly how much evidence the police have. There are letters."

"Love letters— They *were* lovers then?"

"They were in love with each other."

Her face grew grimmer.

"I'm not happy about this, Charles. I don't like Brenda. In the past, I've disliked her very much. I've said sharp things about her. But now—I do feel that I want her to have every chance—every possible chance. Aristide would have wished that. I feel it's up to me to see that—that Brenda gets a square deal."

"And Laurence?"

"Oh, Laurence!" she shrugged her shoulders impatiently. "Men must look after themselves. But Aristide would never forgive us if——" She left the sentence unfinished.

Then she said:

"It must be almost lunch time. We'd better go in."

I explained that I was going up to London.

"In your car?"

"Yes."

"H'm. I wonder if you'd take me with you. I gather we're allowed off the lead now."

"Of course I will, but I believe Magda and Sophia are going up after lunch. You'll be more comfortable with them than in my two-seater."

"I don't want to go with them. Take me with you, and don't say much about it."

I was surprised, but I did as she asked. We did not speak much on the way to town. I asked her where I should put her down.

"Harley Street."

I felt some faint apprehension, but I didn't like to say anything. She continued:

"No, it's too early. Drop me at Debenhams. I can have some lunch there and go to Harley Street afterwards."

"I hope——" I began and stopped.

"That's why I didn't want to go up with Magda. She dramatises things. Lot of fuss."

"I'm very sorry," I said.

"You needn't be. I've had a good life. A very good life." She gave a sudden grin. "And it's not over yet."

XXIII

I HAD NOT seen my father for some days. I found him busy with things other than the Leonides case, and I went in search of Taverner.

Taverner was enjoying a short spell of leisure and was willing to come out and have a drink with me. I congratulated him on having cleared up the case and he accepted my congratulation, but his manner remained far from jubilant.

"Well, that's over," he said. "We've got a case. Nobody can deny we've got a case."

"Do you think you'll get a conviction?"

"Impossible to say. The evidence is circumstantial—it nearly always is in a murder case—bound to be. A lot depends on the impression they make on the jury.'

"How far do the letters go?"

"At first sight, Charles, they're pretty damning. There are references to their life together when her husband's dead. Phrases like—'it won't be long now.' Mind you, defence counsel will try and twist it the other way—the husband was so old that of course they could reasonably expect him to die. There's no actual mention of poisoning—not down in black or white—but there are some passages that could mean that. It depends what judge we get. If it's old Carberry he'll be down on them all through. He's always very righteous about illicit love. I suppose they'll have Eagles or Humphrey Kerr for the defence—Humphrey is magnificent in these cases—but he likes a gallant war record or something of that kind to help him do his stuff. A conscientious objector is going to cramp his style. The question is going to be will the jury like them? You can never tell with juries. You know, Charles, those two are not really sympathetic characters. She's a good-looking woman who married a very old man for his money, and Brown is a neurotic conscientious objector. The

141

crime is so familiar—so according to pattern that you really believe they didn't do it. Of course, they may decide that he did it and she knew nothing about it—or alternately that she did it, and he didn't know about it—or they may decide that they were both in it together."

"And what do you yourself think?" I asked.

He looked at me with a wooden expressionless face.

"I don't think anything. I've turned in the facts and they went to the D.P.P. and it was decided that there was a case. That's all. I've done my duty and I'm out of it. So now you know, Charles."

But I didn't know. I saw that for some reason Taverner was unhappy.

It was not until three days later that I unburdened myself to my father. He himself had never mentioned the case to me. There had been a kind of restraint between us—and I thought I knew the reason for it. But I had to break down that barrier.

"We've got to have this out," I said. "Taverner's not satisfied that those two did it—and you're not satisfied either."

My father shook his head. He said what Taverner had said: "It's out of our hands. There is a case to answer. No question about that."

"But you don't—Taverner doesn't—think that they're guilty?"

"That's for a jury to decide."

"For God's sake," I said, "don't put me off with technical terms. What do you think—both of you—*personally*?"

"My personal opinion is no better than yours, Charles."

"Yes, it is. You've more experience."

"Then I'll be honest with you. I just—don't know!"

"They *could* be guilty?"

"Oh, yes."

"But you don't feel sure that they are?"

My father shrugged his shoulders.

"How can one be sure?"

"Don't fence with me, Dad. You've been sure other times, haven't you? Dead sure? No doubt in your mind at all?"

"Sometimes, yes. Not always."

"I wish to God you were sure this time."

"So do I."

We were silent. I was thinking of those two figures drifting in from the garden in the dusk. Lonely and haunted and afraid. They had been afraid from the start. Didn't that show a guilty conscience?

But I answered myself: "Not necessarily." Both Brenda and Laurence were afraid of life—they had no confidence in themselves, in their ability to avoid danger and defeat, and they could see, only too clearly, the pattern of illicit love leading to murder which might involve them at any moment.

My father spoke, and his voice was grave and kind:

"Come, Charles," he said, "let's face it. You've still got it in your mind, haven't you, that one of the Leonides family is the real culprit?"

"Not really. I only wonder——"

"You do think so. You may be wrong, but you do think so."

"Yes," I said.

"Why?"

"Because"—I thought about it, trying to see clearly—to bring my wits to bear—"because" (yes, that was it), "because they think so themselves."

"They think so themselves? That's interesting. That's very interesting. Do you mean that they all suspect each other, or that they know, actually, who did do it?"

"I'm not sure," I said. "It's all very nebulous and confused. I think—on the whole—that they try to cover up the knowledge from themselves."

My father nodded.

"Not Roger," I said. "Roger wholeheartedly believes it was Brenda and he wholeheartedly wants her hanged. It's—it's a relief to be with Roger, because he's simple and positive, and hasn't any reservations in the back of his mind.

"But the others are apologetic, they're uneasy—they urge me to be sure that Brenda has the best defence—that every possible advantage is given her—why?"

My father answered: "Because they don't really, in their hearts, believe she is guilty . . . Yes, that's sound."

Then he asked quietly:

"Who *could* have done it? You've talked to them all? Who's the best bet?"

"I don't know," I said. "And it's driving me frantic. None of them fits your 'sketch of a murderer' and yet I feel —I do feel—that one of them *is* a murderer."

"Sophia?"

"No. Good God, no!"

"The possibility's in your mind, Charles—yes, it is, don' deny it. All the more potently because you won't acknowledg it. What about the others? Philip?"

"Only for the most fantastic motive."

"Motives can be fantastic—or they can be absurdly slight What's his motive?"

"He is bitterly jealous of Roger—always has been all hi life. His father's preference for Roger drove Philip in upon himself. Roger was about to crash, then the old man heard o it. He promised to put Roger on his feet again. Supposin; Philip learnt that. If the old man died that night ther would be no assistance for Roger. Roger would be down an out. Oh! I know it's absurd——"

"Oh no, it isn't. It's abnormal, but it happens. It's human What about Magda?"

"She's rather childish. She—she gets things out of propor tion. But I would never have thought twice about her being involved if it hadn't been for the sudden way she wanted to pack Josephine off to Switzerland. I couldn't help feeling sh was afraid of something that Josephine knew or migh say——"

"And then Josephine was conked on the head?"

"Well, that couldn't be her mother!"

"Why not?"

"But, Dad, a mother wouldn't——"

"Charles, Charles, don't you ever read the police news? Again and again a mother takes a dislike to one of her children. Only one—she may be devoted to the others. There's some association, some reason, but it's often hard to get at. But when it exists, it's an unreasoning aversion, and it's very strong."

"She called Josephine a changeling," I admitted un willingly.

"Did the child mind?"

"I don't think so."

"Who else is there? Roger?"

"Roger didn't kill his father. I'm quite sure of that."

"Wash out Roger then. His wife—what's her name—— Clemency?"

"Yes," I said. "If she killed old Leonides it was for a very odd reason."

I told him of my conversation with Clemency. I said I thought it possible that in her passion to get Roger away from England she might have deliberately poisoned the old man.

"She persuaded Roger to go without telling his father. Then the old man found out. He was going to back up Associated Catering. All Clemency's hopes and plans were frustrated. And she really does care desperately for Roger—beyond idolatry."

"You're repeating what Edith de Haviland said!"

"Yes. And Edith's another whom I think—might have done it. But I don't know why. I can only believe that for what she considered a good and sufficient reason she might take the law into her own hands. She's that kind of person."

"And she also was very anxious that Brenda should be adequately defended?"

"Yes. That, I suppose, might be conscience. I don't think for a moment that if she did do it, she intended them to be accused of the crime."

"Probably not. But would she knock out the child, Josephine?"

"No," I said slowly. "I can't believe that. Which reminds me that there's something that Josephine said to me that keeps nagging at my mind, and I can't remember what it is. It's slipped my memory. But it's something that doesn't fit in where it should. If only I could remember——"

"Never mind. It will come back. Anything or anyone else on your mind?"

"Yes," I said. "Very much so. How much do you know about infantile paralysis. Its after effects on character, I mean?"

"Eustace?"

"Yes. The more I think about it, the more it seems to me that Eustace might fit the bill. His dislike and resentment against his grandfather. His queerness and moodiness. He's not normal.

"He's the only one of the family who I can see knocking out Josephine quite callously if she knew something about him—and she's quite likely to know. That child knows everything. She writes it down in a little book——"

I stopped.

"Good Lord," I said. "What a fool I am."

145

"What's the matter?"

"I know now what was wrong. We assumed, Taverner and I, that the wrecking of Josephine's room, the frantic search, was for those letters. I thought that she'd got hold of them and that she'd hidden them up in the cistern room. But when she was talking to me the other day she made it quite clear that it was *Laurence* who had hidden them there. She saw him coming out of the cistern room and went snooping around and found the letters. Then, of course, she read them. She would! But she left them where they were."

"Well?"

"Don't you see? *It couldn't have been the letters someone was looking for in Josephine's room.* It must have been something else."

"And that something——"

"Was the little black book she writes down her 'detection' in. That's what someone was looking for! I think, too, that whoever it was didn't find it. I think Josephine still has it. But if so——"

I half rose.

"If so," said my father, "she still isn't safe. Is that what you were going to say?"

"Yes. She won't be out of danger until she's actually started for Switzerland. They're planning to send her there, you know."

"Does she want to go?"

I considered.

"I don't think she does."

"Then she probably hasn't gone," said my father, dryly. "But I think you're right about the danger. You'd better go down there."

"Eustace?" I cried desperately. "Clemency?"

My father said gently:

"To my mind the facts point clearly in one direction. ... I wonder you don't see it yourself. I ..."

Glover opened the door.

"Beg pardon, Mr. Charles, the telephone. Miss Leonides speaking from Swinly Dean. It's urgent."

It seemed like a horrible repetition. Had Josephine again fallen a victim. And had the murderer this time made no mistake ... ?

I hurried to the telephone.

"Sophia? It's Charles here."

Sophia's voice came with a kind of hard desperation in it. Charles, it isn't all over. The murderer is still here."

"What on earth do you mean? What is wrong? Is it —Josephine?"

"It's not Josephine. It's Nannie."

"*Nannie?*"

"Yes, there was some cocoa—Josephine's cocoa, she didn't drink it. She left it on the table. Nannie thought it was a pity to waste it. So she drank it."

"Poor Nannie. Is she very bad?"

Sophia's voice broke.

"Oh, Charles, she's *dead.*"

XXIV

WE WERE back again in the nightmare.

That is what I thought as Taverner and I drove out of London. It was a repetition of our former journey.

At intervals, Taverner swore.

As for me, I repeated from time to time, stupidly, unprofitably: "So it wasn't Brenda and Laurence. It wasn't Brenda and Laurence."

Had I really thought it was? I had been so glad to think it. So glad to escape from other, more sinister, possibilities . . .

They had fallen in love with each other. They had written silly sentimental romantic letters to each other. They had indulged in hopes that Brenda's old husband might soon die peacefully and happily—but I wondered really if they had even acutely desired his death. I had a feeling that the despairs and longings of an unhappy love affair suited them as well or better than commonplace married life together. I didn't think Brenda was really passionate. She was too anaemic, too apathetic. It was romance she craved for. And I thought Laurence, too, was the type to enjoy frustration and vague future dreams of bliss rather than the concrete satisfaction of the flesh.

They had been caught in a trap and, terrified, they had not had the wit to find their way out. Laurence, with incredible stupidity, had not even destroyed Brenda's letters. Presumably Brenda had destroyed his, since they had not been found

And it was not Laurence who had balanced the marble door stop on the wash-house door. It was someone else whose face was still hidden behind a mask.

We drove up to the door. Taverner got out and I followed him. There was a plain clothes man in the hall whom I didn't know. He saluted Taverner and Taverner drew him aside.

My attention was taken by a pile of luggage in the hall. It was labelled and ready for departure. As I looked at it Clemency came down the stairs and through the open door at the bottom. She was dressed in her same red dress with a tweed coat over it and a red felt hat.

"You're in time to say good-bye, Charles," she said.

"You're leaving?"

"We go to London to-night. Our plane goes early to morrow morning."

She was quiet and smiling, but I thought her eyes were watchful.

"But surely you can't go now?"

"Why not?" Her voice was hard.

"With this death——"

"Nannie's death has nothing to do with us."

"Perhaps not. But all the same——"

"Why do you say 'perhaps not'? It *has* nothing to do with us. Roger and I have been upstairs, finishing packing up. We did not come down at all during the time that the cocoa was left on the hall table."

"Can you prove that?"

"I can answer for Roger. And Roger can answer for me."

"No more than that . . . You're man and wife, remember."

Her anger flamed out.

"You're impossible, Charles! Roger and I are going away —to lead our own life. Why on earth should we want to poison a nice stupid old woman who had never done us any harm?"

"It mightn't have been her you meant to poison."

"Still less are we likely to poison a child."

"It depends rather on the child, doesn't it?"

"What do you mean?"

"Josephine isn't quite the ordinary child. She knows a good deal about people. She——"

I broke off. Josephine had emerged from the door leading to the drawing-room. She was eating the inevitable apple, and

148

over its round rosiness her eyes sparkled with a kind of ghoulish enjoyment.

"Nannie's been poisoned," she said. "Just like grandfather. It's awfully exciting, isn't it?"

"Aren't you at all upset about it?" I demanded severely. "You were fond of her, weren't you?"

"Not particularly. She was always scolding me about something or other. She fussed."

"Are you fond of anybody, Josephine?" asked Clemency.

Josephine turned her ghoulish eyes towards Clemency.

"I love Aunt Edith," she said. "I love Aunt Edith very much. And I could love Eustace, only he's always such a beast to me and won't be interested in finding out who did all this."

"You'd better stop finding things out, Josephine," I said. "It isn't very safe."

"I don't need to find out any more," said Josephine. "I know."

There was a moment's silence. Josephine's eyes, solemn and unwinking, were fixed on Clemency. A sound like a long sigh reached my ears. I swung sharply round. Edith de Haviland stood half-way down the staircase—but I did not think it was she who had sighed. The sound had come from behind the door through which Josephine had just come.

I stepped sharply across to it and yanked it open. There was no one to be seen.

Nevertheless I was seriously disturbed. Someone had stood just within that door and had heard those words of Josephine's. I went back and took Josephine by the arm. She was eating her apple and staring stolidly at Clemency. Behind the solemnity there was, I thought, a certain malignant satisfaction.

"Come on, Josephine," I said. "We're going to have a little talk."

I think Josephine might have protested, but I was not standing any nonsense. I ran her along forcibly into her own part of the house. There was a small unused morning room where we could be reasonably sure of being undisturbed. I took her in there, closed the door firmly, and made her sit on a chair. I took another chair and drew it forward so that I faced her. "Now, Josephine," I said, "we're going to have a showdown. What exactly do you know?"

"Lots of things."

"That I have no doubt about. That noddle of yours is probably crammed to overflowing with relevant and irrelevant information. But you know perfectly what I mean. Don't you?"

"Of course I do. *I'm* not stupid."

I didn't know whether the disparagement was for me or the police, but I paid no attention to it and went on:

"You know who put something in your cocoa?"

Josephine nodded.

"You know who poisoned your grandfather?"

Josephine nodded again.

"And who knocked you on the head?"

Again Josephine nodded.

"Then you're going to come across with what you know. You're going to tell me all about it—now."

"Shan't."

"You've got to. Every bit of information you've got or ferret out has got to be given to the police."

"I won't tell the police anything. They're stupid. They thought Brenda had done it—or Laurence. I wasn't stupid like that. I knew jolly well they hadn't done it. I've had an idea who it was all along, and then I made a kind of test —and now I know I'm right."

She finished on a triumphant note.

I prayed to Heaven for patience and started again.

"Listen, Josephine, I dare say you're extremely clever——" Josephine looked gratified. "But it won't be much good to you to be clever if you're not alive to enjoy the fact. Don't you see, you little fool, that as long as you keep your secrets in this silly way you're in imminent danger?"

Josephine nodded approvingly. "Of course I am."

"Already you've had two very narrow escapes. One attempt nearly did for you. The other has cost somebody else their life. Don't you see if you go on strutting about the house and proclaiming at the top of your voice that you know who the killer is, there will be more attempts made —and that either you'll die or somebody else will?"

"In some books person after person is killed," Josephine informed me with gusto. "You end by spotting the murderer because he or she is practically the only person left."

"This isn't a detective story. This is Three Gables, Swinly

Dean, and you're a silly little girl who's read more than is good for her. I'll make you tell me what you know if I have to shake you till your teeth rattle."

"I could always tell you something that wasn't true."

"You could, but you won't. What are you waiting for, anyway?"

"You don't understand," said Josephine. "Perhaps I may never tell. You see, I might—be fond of the person."

She paused as though to let this sink in.

"And if I do tell," she went on, "I shall do it properly. I shall have everybody sitting round, and then I'll go over it all—with the clues, and then I shall say, quite suddenly:

"'And it was *you* ...'"

She thrust out a dramatic forefinger just as Edith de Haviland entered the room.

"Put that core in the waste-paper basket, Josephine," said Edith. "Have you got a handkerchief? Your fingers are sticky. I'm taking you out in the car." Her eyes met mine with significance as she said: "You'll be safer out here for the next hour or so." As Josephine looked mutinous, Edith added: "We'll go into Longbridge and have an ice cream soda."

Josephine's eyes brightened and she said: "Two."

"Perhaps," said Edith. "Now go and get your hat and coat on and your dark blue scarf. It's cold out to-day. Charles, you had better go with her while she gets them. Don't leave her. I have just a couple of notes to write."

She sat down at the desk, and I escorted Josephine out of the room. Even without Edith's warning, I would have stuck to Josephine like a leech.

I was convinced that there was danger to the child very near at hand.

As I finished superintending Josephine's toilet, Sophia came into the room. She seemed rather astonished to see me.

"Why, Charles, have you turned nursemaid? I didn't know you were here."

"I'm going in to Longbridge with Aunt Edith," said Josephine importantly. "We're going to have ice creams."

"Brrr, on a day like this?"

"Ice cream sodas are always lovely," said Josephine. "When you're cold inside, it makes you feel hotter outside."

Sophia frowned. She looked worried, and I was shocked by her pallor and the circles under her eyes.

We went back to the morning room. Edith was just blotting a couple of envelopes. She got up briskly.

"We'll start now," she said. "I told Evans to bring round the Ford."

She swept out to the hall. We followed her.

My eye was again caught by the suitcases and their blue labels. For some reason they aroused in me a vague disquietude.

"It's quite a nice day," said Edith de Haviland, pulling on her gloves and glancing up at the sky. The Ford ten was waiting in front of the house. "Cold—but bracing. A real English autumn day. How beautiful trees look with their bare branches against the sky—and just a golden leaf or two still hanging . . ."

She was silent a moment or two, then she turned and kissed Sophia.

"Good-bye, dear," she said. "Don't worry too much. Certain things have to be faced and endured."

Then she said, "Come, Josephine," and got into the car. Josephine climbed in beside her.

They both waved as the car drove off.

"I suppose she's right, and it's better to keep Josephine out of this for a while. But we've got to make that child tell what she knows, Sophia."

"She probably doesn't know anything. She's just showing off. Josephine likes to make herself look important, you know."

"It's more than that. Do they know what poison it was in the cocoa?"

"They think it's digitalin. Aunt Edith takes digitalin for her heart. She has a whole bottle full of little tablets up in her room. Now the bottle's empty."

"She ought to keep things like that locked up."

"She did. I suppose it wouldn't be difficult for someone to find out where she hid the key."

"Someone? Who?" I looked again at the pile of luggage. I said suddenly and loudly:

"They can't go away. They mustn't be allowed to."

Sophia looked surprised.

"Roger and Clemency? Charles, you don't think——"

"Well, what do *you* think?"

Sophia stretched out her hands in a helpless gesture.

152

"I don't know, Charles," she whispered. "I only know that I'm back—back in the nightmare——"

"I know. Those were the very words I used to myself as I drove down with Taverner."

"Because this is just what a nightmare is. Walking about among people you know, looking in their faces—and suddenly the faces change—and it's not someone you know any longer—it's a stranger—a cruel stranger . . ."

She cried:

"Come outside, Charles—come outside. It's safer outside . . . I'm afraid to stay in this house. . . ."

XXV

WE STAYED in the garden a long time. By a kind of tacit consent, we did not discuss the horror that was weighing upon us. Instead Sophia talked affectionately of the dead woman, of things they had done, and games they had played as children with Nannie—and tales that the old woman used to tell them about Roger and their father and the other brothers and sisters.

"They were her real children, you see. She only came back to us to help during the war when Josephine was a baby and Eustace was a funny little boy."

There was a certain balm for Sophia in these memories and I encouraged her to talk.

I wondered what Taverner was doing. Questioning the household, I suppose. A car drove away with the police photographer and two other men, and presently an ambulance drove up.

Sophia shivered a little. Presently the ambulance left and we knew that Nannie's body had been taken away in preparation for an autopsy.

And still we sat or walked in the garden and talked—our words becoming more and more of a cloak for our real thoughts.

Finally, with a shiver, Sophia said:

"It must be very late—it's almost dark. We've got to go in. Aunt Edith and Josephine haven't come back . . . Surely they ought to be back by now?"

A vague uneasiness woke in me. What had happened? Was

153

Edith deliberately keeping the child away from the Crooked House?

We went in. Sophia drew all the curtains. The fire was lit and the big drawing-room looked harmonious with an unreal air of bygone luxury. Great bowls of bronze chrysanthemums stood on the tables.

Sophia rang and a maid whom I recognised as having been formerly upstairs brought in tea. She had red eyes and sniffed continuously. Also I noticed that she had a frightened way of glancing quickly over her shoulder.

Magda joined us, but Philip's tea was sent in to him in the library. Magda's role was a stiff frozen image of grief. She spoke little or not at all. She said once:

"Where are Edith and Josephine? They're out very late."

But she said it in a preoccupied kind of way.

But I myself was becoming increasingly uneasy. I asked if Taverner were still in the house and Magda replied that she thought so. I went in search of him. I told him that I was worried about Miss de Haviland and the child.

He went immediately to the telephone and gave certain instructions.

"I'll let you know when I have news," he said.

I thanked him and went back to the drawing-room. Sophia was there with Eustace. Magda had gone.

"He'll let us know if he hears anything," I said to Sophia.

She said in a low voice:

"Something's happened, Charles, something *must* have happened."

"My dear Sophia, it's not really late yet."

"What are you bothering about?" said Eustace. "They've probably gone to the cinema."

He lounged out of the room. I said to Sophia: "She may have taken Josephine to a hotel—or up to London. I think she really realised that the child was in danger—perhaps she realised it better than we did."

Sophia replied with a sombre look that I could not quite fathom.

"She kissed me good-bye . . ."

I did not see quite what she meant by that disconnected remark, or what it was supposed to show. I asked if Magda was worried.

"Mother? No, she's all right. She's no sense of time. She's

reading a new play of Vavasour Jones called *The Woman Disposes*. It's a funny play about murder—a female Bluebeard—cribbed from *Arsenic and Old Lace* if you ask me, but it's got a good woman's part, a woman who's got a mania for being a widow."

I said no more. We sat, pretending to read.

It was half-past six when Taverner opened the door and came in. His face prepared us for what he had to say.

Sophia got up.

"Yes?" she said.

"I'm sorry. I've got bad news for you. I sent out a general alarm for the car. A motorist reported having seen a Ford car with a number something like that turning off the main road at Flackspur Heath—through the woods."

"Not—the track to the Flackspur Quarry?"

"Yes, Miss Leonides." He paused and went on. "The car's been found in the quarry. Both the occupants were dead. You'll be glad to know they were killed outright."

"Josephine!" It was Magda standing in the doorway. Her voice rose in a wail. "Josephine . . . My baby."

Sophia went to her and put her arms round her. I said: "Wait a minute."

I had remembered something! Edith de Haviland writing a couple of letters at the desk, going out into the hall with them in her hand.

But they had not been in her hand when she got into the car.

I dashed out into the hall and went to the long oak chest. I found the letters—pushed inconspicuously to the back behind a brass tea-urn.

The uppermost was addressed to Chief-Inspector Taverner.

Taverner had followed me. I handed the letter to him and he tore it open. Standing beside him I read its brief contents.

My expectation is that this will be opened after my death. I wish to enter into no details, but I accept full responsibility for the deaths of my brother-in-law, Aristide Leonides and Janet Rowe, (Nannie). I hereby solemnly declare that Brenda Leonides and Laurence Brown are innocent of the murder of Aristide Leonides. Inquiry of Dr. Michael Chavasse, 783 Harley Street, will confirm that my life could only have been prolonged for a few months. I prefer to take this way out and to spare two innocent people the ordeal of being charged with a murder they did not commit. I am of sound mind and fully conscious of what I write.

Edith Elfrida de Haviland.

As I finished the letter I was aware that Sophia, too, had read it—whether with Taverner's concurrence or not, I don't know.

"*Aunt Edith . . .*" murmured Sophia.

I remembered Edith de Haviland's ruthless foot grinding bindweed into the earth. I remembered my early, almost fanciful, suspicions of her. But why——

Sophia spoke the thought in my mind before I came to it.

"But why Josephine? Why did she take Josephine with her?"

"Why did she do it at all?" I demanded. "What was her motive?"

But even as I said that, I knew the truth. I saw the whole thing clearly. I realised that I was still holding her second letter in my hand. I looked down and saw my own name on it.

It was thicker and harder than the other one. I think I knew what was in it before I opened it. I tore the envelope along and Josephine's little black note-book fell out. I picked it up off the floor—it came open in my hand and I saw the entry on the first page . . .

Sounding from a long way away, I heard Sophia's voice, clear and self-controlled.

"We've got it all wrong," she said. "Edith didn't do it."

"No," I said.

Sophia came closer to me—she whispered:

"It was—Josephine—wasn't it? That was it, Josephine."

Together we looked down on the first entry in the little black book, written in an unformed childish hand:

"*To-day I killed grandfather.*"

XXVI

I WAS TO wonder afterwards that I could have been so blind. The truth had stuck out so clearly all along. Josephine and only Josephine fitted in with all the necessary qualifications. Her vanity, her persistent self-importance, her delight in talking, her reiteration on how clever *she* was, and how stupid the police were.

I had never considered her because she was a child. But children have committed murders, and this particular murder had been well within a child's compass. Her grandfather himself had indicated the precise method—he had practically handed her a blueprint. All she had to do was to avoid leaving fingerprints and the slightest knowledge of detection fiction would teach her that. And everything else had been a mere hotch-potch, culled at random from stock mystery stories. The note-book—the sleuthing—her pretended suspicions, her insistence that she was not going to tell till she was sure. . . .

And finally the attack on herself. An almost incredible performance considering that she might easily have killed herself. But then, childlike, she had never considered such a possibility. She was the heroine. The heroine isn't killed. Yet there had been a clue there—the traces of earth on the seat of the old chair in the wash-house. Josephine was the only person who would have had to climb up on a chair to balance the block of marble on the top of the door. Obviously it had missed her more than once (the dints in the floor) and patiently she had climbed up again and replaced it, handling it with her scarf to avoid fingerprints. And then it had fallen—and she had had a near escape from death.

It had been the perfect set-up—the impression she was aiming for! She was in danger, she "knew something," she had been attacked!

I saw how she had deliberately drawn my attention to her presence in the cistern room. And she had completed the artistic disorder of her room before going out to the wash-house.

But when she had returned from hospital, when she had found Brenda and Laurence arrested, she must have become dissatisfied. The case was over—and she—Josephine, was out of the limelight.

So she stole the digitalin from Edith's room and put it in her own cup of cocoa and left the cup untouched on the hall table.

Did she know that Nannie would drink it? Possibly. From her words that morning, she had resented Nannie's criticisms of her. Did Nannie, perhaps, wise from a life-time of experience with children, suspect? I think that Nannie knew,

157

had always known, that Josephine was not normal. With her precocious mental development had gone a retarded moral sense. Perhaps, too, the various factors of heredity—what Sophia had called the "ruthlessness of the family"—had met together.

She had had an authoritarian ruthlessness of her grandmother's family, and the ruthless egoism of Magda, seeing only her own point of view. She had also presumably suffered, sensitive like Philip, from the stigma of being the unattractive—the changeling child—of the family. Finally, in her very marrow had run the essential crooked strain of old Leonides. She had been Leonides' grandchild, she had resembled him in brain and cunning—but where his love had gone outwards to family and friends, hers had turned inward to herself.

I thought that old Leonides had realised what none of the rest of the family had realised, that Josephine might be a source of danger to others and to herself. He had kept her from school life because he was afraid of what she might do. He had shielded her, and guarded her in the home, and I understood now his urgency to Sophia to look after Josephine.

Magda's sudden decision to send Josephine abroad—had that, too, been due to a fear for the child? Not, perhaps, a conscious fear, but some vague maternal instinct.

And Edith de Haviland? Had she first suspected, then feared—and finally known?

I looked down at the letter in my hand.

Dear Charles. This is in confidence for you—and for Sophia if you so decide. It is imperative that someone should know the truth. I found the enclosed in the disused dog kennel outside the back door. She kept it there. It confirms what I already suspected. The action I am about to take may be right or wrong—I do not know. But my life, in any case, is close to its end, and I do not want the child to suffer as I believe she would suffer if called to earthly account for what she has done.

There is often one of the litter who is "not quite right."

If I am wrong, God forgive me—but I did it out of love. God bless you both.

Edith de Haviland.

I hesitated for only a moment, then I handed the letter

158

to Sophia. Together we again opened Josephine's little black book.

To-day I killed grandfather.

We turned the pages. It was an amazing production. Interesting, I should imagine, to a psychologist. It set out, with such terrible clarity, the fury of thwarted egoism. The motive for the crime was set down, pitifully childish and inadequate.

Grandfather wouldn't let me do bally dancing so I made up my mind I would kill him. Then we should go to London and live and mother wouldn't mind me doing bally.

I give only a few entries. They are all significant.

I don't want to go to Switzerland—I won't go. If mother makes me I will kill her too—only I can't get any poison. Perhaps I could make it with youberries. They are poisonous, the book says so.

Eustace has made me very cross to-day. He says I am only a girl and no use and that it's silly my detecting. He wouldn't think me silly if he knew it was me did the murder.

I like Charles—but he is rather stupid. I have not decided yet who I shall make have done the crime. Perhaps Brenda and Laurence—Brenda is nasty to me—she says I am not all there but I like Laurence—he told me about Charlot Korday—she killed someone in his bath. She was not very clever about it.

The last entry was revealing.

I hate Nannie . . . I hate her . . . I hate her . . . She says I am only a little girl. She says I show off. She's making mother send me abroad . . . I'm going to kill her too —I think Aunt Edith's medicine would do it. If there is another murder, then the police will come back and it will all be exciting again.

Nannie's dead. I am glad. I haven't decided yet where I'll hide the bottle with the little pill things. Perhaps in Aunt Clemency's room—or else Eustace. When I am dead as an old woman I shall leave this behind me addressed to the Chief of Police and they will see what a really great criminal I was.

I closed the book. Sophia's tears were flowing fast.

"Oh, Charles—oh, Charles—it's so dreadful. She's such a little monster—and yet—and yet it's so terribly pathetic."

I had felt the same.

I had liked Josephine . . . I still felt a fondness for

her . . . You do not like anyone less because they have tuberculosis or some other fatal disease. Josephine was, as Sophia had said, a little monster, but she was a pathetic little monster. She had been born with a kink—the crooked child of the little Crooked House.

Sophia asked.

"If—she had lived—what would have happened?"

"I suppose she would have been sent to a reformatory or a special school. Later she would have been released—or possibly certified, I don't know."

Sophia shuddered.

"It's better the way it is. But Aunt Edith—I don't like to think of her taking the blame."

"She chose to do so. I don't suppose it will be made public. I imagine that when Brenda and Laurence come to trial, no case will be brought against them and they will be discharged"

"And you, Sophia," I said, this time on a different note and taking both her hands in mine, "will marry me. I've just heard I'm appointed to Persia. We will go out there together and you will forget the little Crooked House. Your mother can put on plays and your father can buy more books and Eustace will soon go to a university. Don't worry about them any more. Think of me."

Sophia looked at me straight in the eyes.

"Aren't you afraid, Charles, to marry me?"

"Why should I be? In poor little Josephine all the worst of the family came together. In you, Sophia, I fully believe that all that is bravest and best in the Leonides family has been handed down to you. Your grandfather thought highly of you and he seems to have been a man who was usually right. Hold up your head, my darling. The future is ours."

"I will, Charles. I love you and I'll marry you and make you happy." She looked down at the note-book. "Poor Josephine."

"Poor Josephine," I said.

"What's the truth of it, Charles?" said my father.

I never lie to the Old Man.

"It wasn't Edith de Haviland, sir," I said. "It was Josephine."

My father nodded his head gently.

"Yes," he said. "I've thought so for some time. Poor child. . . ."